"Djuna Barnes's 1920s and '30s Paris is on the cusp of leaving behind forever the haute world of Henry James, taken from Proust. That is a world where the better people dine in the Bois, and where open horse-drawn carriages still circle the park . . . Humans suffer and, gay or straight, they break themselves into pieces, blur themselves with drinks and drugs, choose the wrong lover, crucify themselves on their own longings, and, let's not forget, are crucified by a world that fears the stranger—whether in life or in love."

—Jeanette Winterson

"The high priestess of modernism emerges in dark, lyrical tales of disaffection and alienation. With their cosmopolitan settings and points of view, Barnes's mature work displays all the ambiguity, world weariness, and cynicism that distinguish *Nightwood* (1936), her dense, elusive modern masterpiece."

—*Kirkus Reviews*

"Barnes writes of her characters as if they were animals in the pages of a biology textbook, suddenly appearing in a dictionary of Greek gods . . . People are the worshipped or despised creations of a harsh mind. They become things with properties, diseases with symptoms, almost: they are made mythical as we read."

—Gaby Wood, *London Review of Books*

"Miss Barnes has gone beyond Mrs. Woolf's practice of her own theory . . . For Miss Barnes is not even concerned with the immediate in time that fascinated the stream-of-consciousness novelists. In her novel poetry is the bloodstream of the universal organism, a poetry that derives its coherence from the meeting of kindred spirits . . . it is the pattern of life, something that cannot be avoided."

—Alfred Kazin, *New York Times Book Review*

"A cult writer whose melodramatically unhappy life brought her into the Left Bank orbit of expatriate authors ranging from James Joyce to Gertrude Stein, Barnes employed an elliptical, sometimes surrealistic, style as an elaborate screen for the autobiographical sources and raw pain that lie behind much of her work."

—*Publishers Weekly*

I AM ALIEN TO LIFE

SELECTED STORIES

DJUNA BARNES

EDITED AND WITH A FOREWORD BY MERVE EMRE

McNally Editions

New York

McNally Editions
134 Prince St.
New York, NY 10012

ISBN: 978-1-96134-122-7
E-book: 978-1-96134-123-4

Design by Jonathan Lippincott

1   3   5   7   9   10   8   6   4   2

CONTENTS

CONTENTS

FOREWORD

To read Djuna Barnes attentively is to begin to suspect how wretched she must have been. Her themes are love and death, especially in Paris and New York; the corruption of nature by culture; the tainted innocence of children; and the mute misery of beasts. In nearly every other one of her stories, one encounters a man or a woman down on all fours, trembling, weeping, half-mad with lust or torment. In "Spillway," the tubercular Mrs. Julie Anspacher returns from a long stay at a sanatorium with a daughter, the dying child of a dead lover, and tries to explain the nature of her misery to her bewildered husband. "It is a thing beyond the end of everything," she tells him. "It's suffering without a consummation; it's like insufficient sleep; it's like anything without proportion." Yet her suffering fills her with a hysterical joy—with the ecstasy of having become "alien to life." When, at the end of the story, she lowers herself "down, down, down, down" on her hands and knees, one wonders if she will ever get up again.

This is the essential tension of Djuna Barnes's short fiction: her characters may be alien to life, but they are alive—spectacularly, grotesquely alive, and preserved by their illicit desires and obscene thoughts. About these thoughts, they seem to have no choice but to talk torrentially, to strain and to gasp at the monstrosity of life in breathless, broken sentences. There is mystery in their talk—like her contemporaries Mary Butts and Mina Loy, Barnes's language is at once sensational and veiled—but no spirituality. Her characters suffer purely and plainly, with no possibility of grace, no hope of redemption, no transcendence through the power of art or God. Worldly Madame von Bartmann of "Aller et Retour" takes pleasure in informing her timid daughter that life "is filthy; it is also frightful." "There is everything in it," she says, "murder, pain, beauty, disease—death. God is the light the mortal insect kindled, to turn to, and to die by. That is very wise, but it must not be misunderstood." Recoiling from her mother's insistence that she "know *everything*," the daughter marries a government clerk, a man of wealth and incurably dull habits, committing herself to a life of propriety. As Madame von Bartmann takes her leave from the couple, she laments her wasted efforts at enlightening her child. "Ah, how unnecessary!" she sighs.

The world of Barnes's stories is divided between those who speak the truth and those who refuse to hear it. One wonders which is the light and which is the shadow—the knowledge of pain or ignorance? Yet whether her characters accept it or not, suffering is the grounds of existence. "There is something in me that is mournful because it is being," the gynecologist Dr. Katrina Silverstaff cries in "The Doctors," which suggests that, from the beginning, life is pathological; that it is "rotten in virtue and in vice," Madame von Bartmann informs her daughter. For Barnes, life's rottenness eats into us all—virgins and whores, murderers and saints, humans and horses, flowers and vines. Her masochism is relentlessly, obsessively democratic, and it cannot be unraveled from her deep sense of sympathy or her conception of love; the uncommon interest that she demonstrates in any creature, however degenerate, who turns up on the doorstep of her imagination. It would be easy for this talk of suffering to turn brittle or humorless. But Barnes knows when to cue our laughter; Dr. Silverstaff is a fantastic name for a gynecologist.

What explains Barnes? Although I had read and taught her 1936 novel *Nightwood* many times before reading her stories, it had never occurred to me to investigate her life. For a long time, I believed that the strange beauty of her language had bucked my desire for history; I now wonder if I was afraid of what I would discover. My reaction, I later learned, was the opposite of her biographer Phillip Herring's reaction to her writing. "I wanted to teach *Nightwood*, but I felt frustrated by my futile attempts to understand it. Before I could understand the novel," he concluded, "I had to understand Djuna Barnes." She was born on Storm King Mountain in 1892, the daughter of an English woman and a wandering American fiddler and horse breeder, a man who believed in free love and trafficked freely in cruelty. Her home in the Hudson River Valley was filled with his lovers and friends, one or more of whom, Barnes hints in her journals, raped her when she was a teenager. For a time, she lived with her grandmother, with whom she had, at the least, an appallingly intimate relationship. When she returned to her father's home, he turned Barnes, her sisters and brothers, and her mother out and refused to support them. She moved to New York, then to Paris in 1921, where she ran around with Eliot, Pound, and Stein, and had the shattering love affair with

Thelma Wood that she drew on for *Nightwood*. She did not return to New York until 1939, alone and destitute. When she died in 1982, she had published nearly nothing for forty years. Here was a life forged in a constant, unfathomable agony, irradiating any milder emotions.

The concentration of pain seems to have led to a notably concentrated aesthetic. We can count on one hand her recurrent settings and detailed scenes. There is a city, glittering and squalid. Or there is the sinister quiet of the countryside, with one or two well-bred horses in the stable. Inside a house, there are whips of rich leather and a menagerie of decorative objects, "Venetian glasses and bowls of onyx, silks, cushions and perfumes." No doubt Barnes borrows many of her furnishings from the writers of the fin de siècle. But, in her hands, their decadence turns jagged, elliptical, and emphatically cosmopolitan, with characters speaking in tuneful snatches of English, German, Russian, and French.

We can count on the other hand the characters on whom Barnes lavishes her attention. There are men, some melancholy and philosophical, others sensual, contemptuous. In her most chilling story, "Oscar," the former type is represented by Oliver Kahn, who "had an odor about him of the rather recent cult of the 'terribly good'"; the latter by Ulric Straussmann, "the type who can turn the country, with a single gesture, into a brothel." There is often a woman of wealth or noble title, who, though no longer young, burns with a late-blooming, ill-fated love, like Princess Frederica Rholinghausen of "The Passion" or Madame Boliver of "Indian Summer." Sometimes, there is a child or a childlike figure who seeks to penetrate the secrets of the adult world, as in "A Boy Asks a Question" or "The Rabbit." Expecting compassion or guidance, the child is initiated into the horrors of sex and death.

The story "The Perfect Murder" seems to parody Barnes's fixation on perverse human specimens. Professor Anatol Profax, a dialectologist, is on a quest to find a truly original human being. He meets a trapeze artist on the street, a woman in flowing black who speaks brightly and manically, in riddles. She tells him that she regularly dies and returns to life, each time as a new trauma, a testament to the many depravities of modern civilization: "People adore me—after a long time, after I have told them how beastly they are—weak and sinful." Perhaps because he is maddened by her, perhaps to call her bluff, the professor slits her throats and packs her body into his leather trunk. The body disappears, only to reappear later that day in the taxi next to his. "Lost, lost . . . something extraordinary . . . I've let it slip right through my fingers . . ." he thinks. One can sense in Barnes's fiction the desire to never let an extraordinary creature slip through her grasp.

Plot is not Barnes's strength, although it is difficult to know whether its construction simply fails to hold her interest or because, in the end, all plots—all lives—dead-end in the same revelations, the same drives. "I love, I fear, I hunger, I die," Professor Profax lists them. She is more interested in how these drives can turn a person into something more and less powerful than an ordinary human being. Consider Freda Buckler of the story "A Night Among the Horses," who has "a battery for a heart and the body of a toy." Or consider Madame Boliver, who "lent a plastic embodiment to all hitherto unembodied things. She was like some rare wood, carved into a melting form—she breathed abruptly as one who has been dead for a half a century." Love envelopes her characters like a second skin. Fear dyes the very fibers of their being. At their most sensitive, Barnes's tropes and figures—the rare wood, the battery-operated heart—erode any meaningful distinctions between mind and matter, person and thing. At its crudest, her fiction degrades into racial mythologies. (A character presents "vivid streaks of German lust." Another is "a hot melancholy Jew.") Yet encountering Djuna Barnes's finest characters is like bumping into something hard and heaving in the dark and not being able to discern whether it is a person, an animal, a piece of furniture, or another entity entirely.

Most of the stories are told in the third person by a narrator who possesses a profound understanding of the human condition, an understanding that is hinted at, but never revealed. Four of the stories are first-person soliloquies: "Cassation" (initially called "A Little Girl Tells a Story to a Lady"), "The Grande Malade" ("The Little Girl Continues"), "Dusie," and "Behind the Heart." Their narrators speak with urgency of violent, unrequited love, mostly between women who are "'*tragique*' and '*triste*' and 'tremendous' all at once." Their compulsion to narrate is borne of the desire to remember a past that everyone else would rather forget. "Yes, even now the story had begun to fade with me; it is so in Paris; France eats her own history, *n'est-ce-pas*, madame?" the narrator of "Dusie" asks. The listeners in these stories never respond. Are they bored? Amused? One wonders if they exist at all, or if the little girls are speaking to themselves, trying to keep their own company in the heart of the night.

The last of the soliloquies, "Behind the Heart," is a love story about a man and woman who are briefly together, then separate. Its emotions are keyed to a much lower pitch than the rest of the collection. Its language is simpler and more affecting. It is my favorite, although my attachment to it is a source of both disappointment and relief to me: disappointment that I am not, at this moment, sufficiently estranged from life to feel the truth of her other stories in the absolute depths of my being; relief for the same reason. This estrangement was, for Barnes, the cost of living. For her readers, it is the price of admission to her world. How many of us are willing to pay it? Do we have a choice?

Merve Emre
New Haven, 2024

I AM ALIEN TO LIFE

A NIGHT AMONG THE HORSES

Toward dusk, in the summer of the year, a man in evening dress, carrying a top hat and a cane, crept on hands and knees through the underbrush bordering the pastures of the Buckler estate. His wrists hurt him from holding his weight and he sat down. Sticky ground-vines fanned out all about him; they climbed the trees, the posts of the fence, they were everywhere. He peered through the thickly tangled branches and saw, standing against the darkness, a grove of white birch shimmering like teeth in a skull.

He could hear the gate grating on its hinge as the wind clapped. His heart moved with the movement of the earth. A frog puffed forth its croaking immemorial cry; the man struggled for breath, the air was heavy and hot; he was nested in astonishment.

He wanted to drowse off; instead, he placed his hat and cane beside him, straightening his coat tails, lying out on his back, waiting. Something quick was moving the ground. It began to shake with sudden warning, and he wondered if it was his heart.

A lamp in the far away window winked as the boughs swung against the wind; the odor of crushed grasses mingling with the faint reassuring smell of dung, fanned up and drawled off to the north; he opened his mouth, drawing in the ends of his moustache.

The tremor lengthened, it ran beneath his body and tumbled away into the earth.

He sat upright. Putting on his hat, he braced his cane against the ground between his outthrust legs. Now he not only felt the trembling of the earth but caught the muffled horny sound of hooves smacking the turf, as a friend strikes the back of a friend, hard, but without malice. They were on the near side now as they took the curve of the Willow Road. He pressed his forehead against the bars of the fence.

The soft menacing sound deepened as heat deepens; the horses, head-on, roared by him, their legs rising and falling like savage needles taking purposeless stitches.

He saw their bellies pitching from side to side, racking the bars of the fence as they swung past. On his side of the barrier, he rose up running, following, gasping. His foot caught in the trailing pine, and he pitched forward, striking his head on a stump as he went down. Blood trickled from his scalp. Like a red mane it ran into his eyes, and he stroked it back with the knuckles of his hand, as he put on his hat. In this position the pounding hoofs shook him like a child on a knee.

Presently he searched for his cane; he found it snared in the fern. A wax Patrick-pipe brushed against his cheek, he ran his tongue over it, snapping it in two. Move as he would, the grass was always under him, crackling with twigs and cones. An acorn fell out of the soft dropping powders of the wood. He took it up, and as he held it between finger and thumb, his mind raced over the scene back there with the mistress of the house, for what else could one call Freda Buckler but "the mistress of the house," that small fiery woman, with a battery for a heart and the body of a toy, who ran everything, who purred, saturated with impudence, with a mechanical buzz that ticked away her humanity.

He blew down his moustache. Freda, with that aggravating floating yellow veil! He told her it was "aggravating," he told her that it was "shameless," and stood for nothing but temptation. He puffed out his cheeks, blowing at her as she passed. She laughed, stroking his arm, throwing her head back, her nostrils scarlet to the pit. They had ended by riding out together, a boot's length apart, she no bigger than a bee on a bonnet. In complete misery he had dug down on his spurs, and she: "Gently, John, gently!" showing the edges of her teeth in the wide distilling mouth. "You can't be ostler *all* your life. Horses!" she snorted. "I like horses, but—" He had lowered his crop. "There are other things. You simply can't go on being a groom forever, not with a waist like that, and you know it. I'll make a gentleman out of you. I'll step you up from being a 'thing.' You will see, you will enjoy it."

He had leaned over and lashed at her boot with his whip. It caught her at the knee, the foot flew up in its stirrup, as though she were dancing.

And the little beast was delighted! They trotted on a way, and they trotted back. He helped her to dismount, and she sailed off, trailing the yellow veil, crying back:

"You'll love it!"

Before they had gone on like this for more than a month (bowling each other over in the spirit, wringing each other this way and that, hunter and hunted) it had become a game without any pleasure; debased lady, debased ostler, on the wings of vertigo.

What was she getting him into? He shouted, bawled, cracked whip—what did she figure she wanted? The kind of woman who can't tell the truth; truth ran out and away from her as though her veins wore pipettes, stuck in by the devil; and drinking, he swelled, and pride had him, it floated him off. He saw her standing behind him in every mirror, she followed him from showpiece to showpiece, she fell in beside him, walked him, hand under elbow.

"You will rise to governor-general—well, to inspector—"

"Inspector!"

"As you like, say master of the regiment—say cavalry officer. Horses, too, leather, whips—"

"O my God."

She almost whinnied as she circled on her heels:

"With a broad, flat, noble chest," she said, "you'll become a pavement of honors . . . Mass yourself. You will leave affliction—"

"Stop it!" he shouted. "I *like* being common."

"With a quick waist like that, the horns will miss you."

"What horns?"

"The dilemma."

"I *could* stop you, all over, if I wanted to."

She was amused. "Man in a corner?" she said.

She tormented him, she knew it. She tormented him with her objects of "culture." One knee on an ottoman, she would hold up and out, the most delicate miniature, ivories cupped in her palm, tilting them from the sun, saying: "But look, look!"

He put his hands behind his back. She aborted that. She asked him to hold ancient missals, volumes of fairy tales, all with handsome tooling, all bound in corded russet. She spread maps, and with a long hatpin dragging across mountains and ditches, pointed to "just where she had been." Like a dry snail the point wandered the coast, when abruptly, sticking the steel in, she cried *Borgia!* and stood there, jangling a circle of ancient keys.

His anxiety increased with curiosity. *If* he married her— after he *had* married her, what then? Where would he be after he had satisfied her crazy whim? What would she make of him in the end; in short, what would she leave of him? Nothing, absolutely nothing, not even his horses. He'd be a damned fool for you. He wouldn't fit in anywhere after Freda, he'd be neither what he was nor what he had been; he'd be a *thing*, half standing, half crouching, like those figures under the roofs of historic buildings, the halt position of the damned.

He had looked at her often without seeing her; after a while he began to look at her with great attention. Well, well! Really a small mousy woman, with fair pretty hair that fell like an insect's feelers into the nape of her neck, moving when the wind moved. She darted and bobbled about too much, and always with the mindless intensity of a mechanical toy kicking and raking about the floor.

And she was always a step or two ahead of him, or stroking his arm at arm's length, or she came at him in a gust, leaning her sharp little chin on his shoulder, floating away slowly—only to be stumbled over when he turned.

On this particular day he had caught her by the wrist, slewing her around. This once, he thought to himself, this once I'll ask her straight out for truth; a direct shot might dislodge her.

"Miss Freda, just a moment. You know I haven't a friend in the world. You know positively that I haven't a person to whom I can go and get an answer to any question of any sort. So then, just what *do* you want me for?"

She blushed to the roots of her hair. "Girlish! are you going to be girlish?" She looked as if she were going to scream, her whole frame buzzed, but she controlled herself and drawled with lavish calm:

"Don't be nervous. Be patient. You will get used to everything. You'll even like it. There's nothing so enjoyable as climbing."

"And then?"

"Then everything will slide away, stable and all." She caught the wings of her nose in the pinching folds of a lace handkerchief. "Isn't that a destination?"

The worst of all had been the last night, the evening of the masked ball. She had insisted on his presence. "Come," she said, "just as you are, and be our whipper-in." That was the final blow, the unpardonable insult. He had obeyed, except that he did not come "just as he was." He made an elaborate toilet; he dressed for evening, like any ordinary gentleman; he was the only person present therefore who was not "in dress," that is, in the accepted sense.

On arrival he found most of the guests tipsy. Before long he himself was more than a little drunk and horrified to find that he was dancing a minuet, stately, slow, with a great soft puff-paste of a woman, showered with sequins, grunting in cascades of plaited tulle. Out of this embrace he extricated himself, slipping on the bare spots of the rosin-powdered floor, to find Freda coming at him with a tiny glass of cordial which she poured into his open mouth; at that point he was aware that he had been gasping for air.

He came to a sudden stop. He took in the whole room with his frantic glance. There in the corner sat Freda's mother with her cats. She always sat in corners, and she always sat with cats. And there was the rest of the cast—cousins, nephews, uncles, aunts. The next moment, the *galliard*. Freda, arms up, hands, palm out, elbows buckled in at the breast, a praying mantis, was all but tooth to tooth with him. Wait! He stepped free, and with the knob end of his cane, he drew a circle in the rosin clear around her, then backward went through the French windows.

He knew nothing after that until he found himself in the shrubbery, sighing, his face close to the fence, peering in. He was with his horses again; he was where he belonged again. He could hear them tearing up the sod, galloping about as though in their own ballroom, and oddest of all, at this dark time of the night.

He began drawing himself under the lowest bar, throwing his hat and cane in before him, panting as he crawled. The black stallion was now in the lead. The horses were taking the curve in the Willow Road that ran into the farther pasture, and through the dust they looked faint and enormous.

On the top of the hill, four had drawn apart and were standing, testing the weather. He would catch one, mount

I AM ALIEN TO LIFE

one, he would escape! He was no longer afraid. He stood up, waving his hat and cane and shouting.

They did not seem to know him, and they swerved past him and away. He stared after them, almost crying. He did not think of his dress, the white shirt front, the top hat, the waving stick, his abrupt rising out of the dark, their excitement. Surely, they must know him—in a moment.

Wheeling, manes up, nostrils flaring, blasting out steam as they came on, they passed him in a whinnying flood, and he damned them in horror, but what he shouted was "Bitch!" and found himself swallowing fire from his heart, lying on his face, sobbing, "I *can* do it, damn everything, I can get on with it; I can make my mark!"

The upraised hooves of the first horse missed him, the second did not.

Presently the horses drew apart, nibbling and swishing their tails, avoiding a patch of tall grass.

THE VALET

The fields about Louis-Georges' house grew green in very early spring, leaving the surrounding countryside to its melancholy gray, for Louis-Georges was the only farmer who sowed his fields to rye.

Louis-Georges was a small man with a dark oval face that burned like a Goya and supported a long raking nose in which an hoar-frost of hair bristled. His arms swung their stroke ahead of his legs; his whole person knew who he was—that sort.

He had fierce pride in everything he did, even when not too well executed, not too well comprehended; he himself was so involved in it.

Sometimes standing in the yard, breathing the rich air, nose up, he enjoyed his lands utterly, rubbing the fingers of one hand with the fingers of the other, or waving the hands above the horns of his cattle where, in buzzing loops, flies hung, or slapping the haunches of his racers, saying to the trainer: "There's more breeding in the rump of one of these, than any butt in the stalls of Westminster!"—pretending that he understood all points from muzzle to hoof—in short, a man who all but had a "hand in being."

Sometimes he and Vera Sovna would play hide-and-seek about the grain bins and through the mounds of hay, she in her long flounces and high heels, screaming and leaping among the rakes and flails.

Once Louis-Georges caught a rat, bare hand, and with such skill that it could not use its teeth. He disguised his elation, showing her how it was done, pretending it a cunning he had learned in order to protect the winter grain.

Vera Sovna was a tall creature with thin shoulders which she shrugged as if the blades were too heavy. She usually dressed in black, and she laughed a good part of the time in a rather high key.

She had been the great friend of Louis-Georges' mother, but since the mother's death she had, by her continued intimacy, fallen into disrepute. It was whispered that she was "something" to Louis-Georges. When the landholders saw her enter his house, they could not contain themselves until they saw her leave it; if she came out holding her skirts carefully above her ankles, they found the roofs of their mouths with disapproving tongues; if she walked slowly, dragging her dress, they would say: "What a dust she brings up in the driveway!"

If she knew anything of their feelings, she did not show it. Driving through the town, turning neither to right nor left, she passed right through the market square, looking at nobody, but obviously delighted with the rosy bunches of flowers, the bright tumble of yellow squash and green cucumbers, the fruits piled in orderly heaps on the stands. But on the rare occasions when Louis-Georges accompanied her, she would cross her legs at the knee, or lean forward, or shake a finger at him, or turn her head from side to side, or lean back laughing.

Sometimes she visited the maids' quarters to play with Leah's child, a little creature with bandy legs and frail neck, who thrust out his stomach for her to pat.

The maids, Berthe and Leah, were well-built complacent women with serene blue eyes, fine teeth and round firm busts that flourished like pippins. They went about their duties chewing stalks of rye and salad leaves, reefing with their tongues.

In her youth Leah had evidently done something for which she now prayed at intervals, usually before a wooden Christ, hanging from a beam in the barn, who was so familiar that she did not notice Him until, sitting down to milk, she raised her eyes; then, putting her forehead against the cow's belly, she prayed, the milk splashing over her big knuckles and wasting into the ground, until Berthe came to help her carry the pails, when she would remark, "We are going to have rain."

Vera Sovna spent hours in the garden, the child crawling after her, leaving the marks of his small hands, wet with saliva, on the dusty leaves; digging up young vegetable roots with such sudden ease that he would fall on his back, blinking up at the sun.

The two maids, the valet Vanka, and Louis-Georges were the household, except when augmented by the occasional visits of Louis-Georges' aunts, Myra and Ella.

Vanka was Russian. He bit his nails. He wore his clothes badly, as though he had no time for more than the master's neatness. His rich yellow hair was disheveled though pomaded, his eyebrows shaggy and white. His eyes, when he raised their heavy lids, were gentle and intelligent. He was absolutely devoted.

Louis-Georges would say to him, "Now, Vanka, tell me again what it was they did to you when you were a boy."

"They shot my brother," Vanka would answer, pulling at his forelock. "They shot him for a 'red.' They threw him into prison with my father. Then one day my sister, who took them their food in two pails, heard a noise; it sounded like a shot and that day father returned only one pail, and they say he returned it like a person looking over his shoulder." Vanka told that story often, sometimes adding with a sigh, "My sister, who had been a handsome woman (the students used to visit her just to hear her talk)—became bald—overnight."

After such confidences, Louis-Georges would shut himself up in his study where, in a large scrawling hand, he wrote to his aunts. Sometimes he would put in a phrase or two about Vanka.

Sometimes Vera Sovna would come in to watch, lifting her ruffles, raising her brows. If Vanka was present they would stare each other down, she with her back to the fireplace, her heels apart, saying:

"Come, come, that is enough!" adding, "Vanka, take his pen away."

Louis-Georges went on, smiling and grunting, but never lifting his hand from his written page. As for Vanka, he simply stood catching the pages as they were finished.

Finally with a loud scrape and a great shove, Louis-Georges would push back his chair and standing up would say, "Now, let us have tea."

In the end he fell into a slow illness. It attacked his limbs; he was forced to walk with a cane. He complained of his heart, but he persisted in going out to look at the horses, and to amuse Vera Sovna he would slash at the flies with his stick, enjoying the odor of milk and dung.

He had plans for the haying, for getting in the crops, but he had to give over to the farm hands who, left to themselves, wandered off at any odd hour, to their own acres, to their own broken fences.

Six months later Louis-Georges took to his bed.

The aunts came, testing the rate of decay with their leathery noses, as they portioned out paregoric, like women in charge of a baby, remarking to each other with surprise, "He never used to be like this," easing the velvet straps that bit into their shoulder flesh, peering at each other, from either side of his bed.

They were afraid of meeting Vera Sovna. Their position was difficult. Having been on friendly terms with her while Louis-Georges' mother was alive, they felt that once the old lady was dead, they had to increase in dignity and reserve. Then, too, the townsfolk seemed to have turned against Vera. Still, the aunts did not wish to be too harsh, so they left Louis-Georges' bedside for an hour every evening that Vera Sovna might come to see him, and Vera Sovna came, creeping softly and saying, "Oh, my *dear*!" She would tell him stories, told before, all about her own life, as if that life, not yet spent, might be of help. She told him of her week in London, of a visit to The Hague; of adventures with hotel keepers in impossible inns, and sometimes, leaning close to him, he thought he heard her weeping.

But in spite of this—the illness and the tension in the air—Vera Sovna seemed strangely gay.

During the foundering of Louis-Georges, Leah and Berthe served as nurses, changing his sheets, turning him over to rub him with oil and alcohol, crossing themselves and giving him the spoon.

The valet stood at the foot of the bed trying not to cough or sigh or annoy his master in any way. But sometimes he would fall asleep holding to the bedpost, and wake to dreams of the "revolution," a dream which faded as he caught himself.

Vera Sovna had taken to dining with the girls in the kitchen, a long bare room that pleased her. From the window one could see the orchard and the pump and the long easy slope of the meadow. From the beams braided onions and smoked meats dangled over the long table, strewn with a thin snow of flour, and hot loaves of new bread.

The girls accepted Vera Sovna's company cheerfully. When she went away, they cleared the board, talking of other things, sharpening knives, forgetting.

The matters of the estate went on as usual. Nothing suffered because of the master's infirmity. Crops ripened; the haying season passed; the orchard sounded with the thud of falling fruit. Louis-Georges ripened into death, detached, as if he had never been. About Vera Sovna there was a quiet brilliance. She tended the medicine bottles as though they were musical intervals; she arranged him bouquets as though they were tributes. And Vanka?

There was the one who took on utter anguish, he bent under the shortening shadow of his master as one at last permitted the use of grief for himself.

Myra and Ella in shock, shook crumbs from their laps, sending each other in to visit Louis-Georges, and pretending, each to the other, he was much improved. It was not that they were afraid he might die, they were afraid they were not prepared.

When the doctor arrived, they shifted their uncertainty. They rushed about getting subscriptions filled, spoons polished; they closed their eyes, sitting on either side of his bed, picturing him already shriven and translated, in order to find pleasure in opening their eyes to find him just as usual.

When they knew that he was dying indeed, the aunts could not keep from touching him. They tried to cover him up in those parts that too plainly exposed the rate of his departure; the thin arms, the damp pulsing spot in the neck, the fallen pit of his stomach. They fondled his knuckles and generally drove the doctor and the new nurse frantic. At last, in desperation, Myra, eluding everyone, knelt by Louis-Georges and stroked his face. Death did not seem to be anywhere; that is, it did not seem to stay in one place, but with her caresses, seemed to move from quarter to quarter. At this point, she was locked out with her sister. They wandered up and down the hall, afraid to speak, unable to cry, passing each other, bracing their palms against the walls.

Then when Louis-Georges did die, there was the problem of Vera Sovna. However, they soon forgot her, trying to follow the instructions left by the dead man. Louis-Georges had seen to it that everything should go on as usual; he would not interrupt the seasons, he had "planned" next year.

The hens praised their eggs as usual, as usual the stables resounded with good spirits. The fields shed their very life upon the earth, and Vanka folded and put away the dead man's clothes.

When the undertaker arrived, Vanka would not let him touch the body. He washed and dressed it himself. It was he who laid Louis-Georges in the shining coffin that smelled like violin rosin; it was he who banked the flowers, and he who finally left the scene, on the whole flat of his suddenly clumsy feet. He went to his room and shut the door.

He paced. It seemed to him that he had left something undone. He loved service and order; he loved Louis-Georges who had made service necessary and order desirable. This made him rub his palms together, holding them close to his sighing mouth, as if the sound might teach him some secret of silence. Of course, Leah had made a scene, hardly to be wondered at, considering. She had brought her baby in, dropping him beside the body, giving her first order: "You can play together, now, for a minute."

Vanka had not interfered. The child had been too frightened to disturb the arranged excellence of Louis-Georges' leavetaking, and both the child and mother soon left the room in stolid calm. Vanka could hear them descend to the lower parts of the house, the deliberate thump of Leah, the quick clatter of the child.

Walking to his room, Vanka could hear the trees beating the wind; an owl called from the barn, a mare whinnied, stomped and dropped her head back into her bin. Vanka opened the window. He thought he caught the sound of feet on the pebbled border that rounded the hydrangea bushes; a faint perfume, such as arose from the dancing flounces of Vera Sovna's dress seemed to hang in the air. Irritated, he turned away; then he heard her calling.

"Vanka," she said, "come, my foot is caught in the vine."

Her face, with its open mouth came up above the sill, and the next moment she jumped into the room. And there they stood, looking at each other. They had never been alone before. He did not know what to do.

She was a little disheveled; twigs clung to the flounces of her skirts. She raised both shoulders and sighed; she reached out her hand and said his name.

"Vanka."

He moved away from her, staring.

"Vanka," she repeated, and came close to him, leaning on his arm. With great simplicity she said, "You must tell me everything."

"I'll tell you," he answered automatically.

"Look, your hands!" Suddenly she dropped her head into his palms. He shivered; he drew his hands away.

"Oh, look, you fortunate man!" she cried. "Most fortunate man, most elected Vanka! He let you touch him, close, close, near the skin, near the heart. You knew how he looked, how he stood, how the ankle went into the foot!"— he had ceased to hear her, he was so astonished—"his shoulders, how they set. You dressed and undressed him. You knew him, all of him for years. Tell me—tell me, what was he like?"

He turned. "I will tell you," he said, "if you are still, if you will sit down, if you are quiet."

She sat down: she watched him with great joy.

"His arms were too long," he said, "but you know that, you could see that, but beautiful; and his back, his spine, tapering slender, full of breeding—"

NO MAN'S MARE

Pauvla Agrippa had died that afternoon at three; now she lay with quiet hands crossed a little below her fine breast with its transparent skin showing the veins as filmy as old lace, purple veins that were now only a system of charts indicating the pathways where her life once flowed.

Her small features were angular with that repose which she had often desired. She had not wanted to live, because she did not mind death. There were no candles about her where she lay, nor any flowers. She had said quite logically to her sisters: "Are there any candles and flowers at a birth?" They saw the point, but regretted the philosophy, for buying flowers would have connected them with Pauvla Agrippa, in this, her new adventure.

Pauvla Agrippa's hair lay against her cheeks like pats of plaited butter; the long golden ends tucked in and wound about her head and curved behind her neck. Pauvla Agrippa had once been complimented on her fine black eyes and this yellow hair of hers, and she had smiled and been quite pleased, but had drawn attention to the fact that she had also another quite remarkable set of differences—her small thin arms with their tiny hands and her rather long narrow feet.

She said that she was built to remain standing; now she could rest.

Her sister, Tasha, had been going about all day, praying to different objects in search of one that would give her comfort, though she was not so much grieved as she might have been, because Pauvla Agrippa had been so curious about all this.

True, Agrippa's husband seemed lost, and wandered about like a restless dog, trying to find a spot that would give him relief as he smoked.

One of Pauvla's brothers was playing on the floor with Pauvla's baby. This baby was small and fat and full of curves. His arms curved above his head, and his legs curved downward, including his picture book and rattle in their oval. He shouted from time to time at his uncle, biting the buttons on his uncle's jacket. This baby and this boy had one thing in common—a deep curiosity—a sense that somewhere that curiosity would be satisfied. They had all accomplished something. Pauvla Agrippa and her husband and her sister and the boy and Pauvla's baby, but still there was incompleteness about everything.

Nothing was ever done; there wasn't such a thing as rest, that was certain, for the sister still felt that her prayers were not definite, the husband knew he would smoke again after lunch, the boy knew he was only beginning something, as the baby also felt it, and Pauvla Agrippa herself, the seemingly most complete, had yet to be buried. Her body was confronted with the eternal necessity of change.

It was all very sad and puzzling, and rather nice too. After all, atoms were the only things that had imperishable existence, and therefore were the omnipotent quality and quantity—God should be recognized as something that was everywhere in millions, irrevocable and ineradicable— one single great thing has always been the prey of the million little things. The beasts of the jungle are laid low by the insects. Yes, she agreed that everything was multiple that counted. Pauvla was multiple now, and some day they would be also. This was the reason that she wandered from room to room touching things, vases, candlesticks, tumblers, knives, forks, the holy pictures and statues and praying to each of them, praying for a great thing, to many presences.

A neighbor from across the way came to see them while Pauvla's brother was still playing with the baby. This man was a farmer, once upon a time, and liked to remember it, as city-bred men in the country like to remember New York and its sophistication.

He spent his summers, however, in the little fishing village where the sisters, Pauvla and Tasha, had come to know him. He always spoke of "going toward the sea." He said that there was something more than wild about the ocean; it struck him as being a little unnatural, too.

He came in now grumbling and wiping his face with a coarse red handkerchief, remarking on the "catch" and upon the sorrow of the house of Agrippa, all in the one breath.

"There's a touch of damp in the air," he said, sniffing, his nose held back so that his small eyes gleamed directly behind it. "The fish have been bad catching and no-man's-mare is going up the headlands, her tail stretched straight out."

Tasha came forward with cakes and tea and paused, praying over them also, still looking for comfort. She was a small woman, with a round, wrinkled forehead and the dark eyes of her sister; today she felt inconvenienced because she could not understand her own feelings—once or twice she had looked upon the corpse with resentment because it had done something to Pauvla; however, she was glad to see the old man, and she prayed to him silently also, to see if it would help. Just what she prayed for she could not tell; the words she used were simple: "What is it, what is it?" over and over with her own childhood prayers to end with.

She had a great deal of the quietness of this village about her, the quietness that is in the roaring of the sea and the wind, and when she sighed it was like the sound made of great waters running back to sea between the narrow sides of little stones.

It was here that she, as well as her brothers and sisters, had been born. They fished in the fishing season and sold to the market at one-eighth of the market price, but when the markets went so low that selling would put the profits down for months, they turned the nets over and sent the fish back to sea.

Today Tasha was dressed in her ball-gown; she had been anticipating a local gathering that evening and then Pauvla Agrippa got her heart attack and died. This dress was low about the shoulders, with flounces of taffeta, and the sea-beaten face of Tasha rose out of its stiff elegance like a rock from heavy moss. Now that she had brought the cakes and tea, she sat listening to this neighbor as he spoke French to her younger brother.

When they spoke in this strange language, she was always surprised to note that their voices became unfamiliar to her—she could not have told which was which, or if they were themselves at all. Closing her eyes, she tried to see if this would make any difference, and it didn't. Then she slowly raised her small plump hands and pressed them to her ears—this was better, because now she could not tell that it was French that they were speaking, it was sound only and might have been anything, and again she sighed, and was glad that they were less strange to her; she could not bear this strangeness today, and wished they would stop speaking in a foreign tongue.

"What are you saying?" she inquired, taking the teacup in one hand, keeping the other over her ear.

"Talking about the horse," he said, and went on.

Again, Tasha became thoughtful. This horse that they were speaking about had been on the sands, it seemed to her, for as long as she could remember. It was a wild thing belonging to nobody. Sometimes in a coming storm, she had seen it standing with its head out toward the waters, its mane flying in the light air, and its thin sides fluttering with the beating of its heart.

It was old now, with sunken flanks and knuckled legs; it no longer stood straight—and the hair about its nose had begun to turn gray. It never interfered with the beach activities, and on the other hand it never permitted itself to be touched. Early in her memory of this animal, Tasha had tried to stroke it, but it had started, arched its neck and backed away from her with hurried jumping steps. Many of the ignorant fisherfolk had called it the sea horse and also "no-man's-mare." They began to fear it, and several of them thought it a bad omen.

Tasha knew better—sometimes it would be down upon the pebbly part of the shore, its head laid flat as though it were dead, but no one could approach within fifty feet without its instantly leaping up and standing with its neck thrust forward and its brown eyes watching from beneath the coarse lashes.

In the beginning people had tried to catch it and make it of use. Gradually everyone in the village had made the attempt; not one of them had ever succeeded.

The large black nostrils were always wet, and they shook as though some one was blowing through them—great nostrils like black flowers.

This mare was old now and did not get up so often when approached. Tasha had been as near to it as ten paces, and Pauvla Agrippa had once approached so near that she could see that its eyes were failing, that a thin mist lay over its right eyeball, so that it seemed to be flirting with her, and this made her sad and she hurried away, and she thought, "The horse had its own defense; when it dies it will be so horrifying perhaps that not one of us will approach it." Though many had squabbled about which of them should have its long, beautiful tail.

Pauvla Agrippa's husband had finished his cigar and came in now, bending his head to get through the low casement. He spoke to the neighbor a few moments and then sat down beside his sister-in-law.

He began to tell her that something would have to be done with Pauvla and added that they would have to manage to get her over to the undertaker's at the end of the headland, but that they had no means of conveyance. Tasha thought of this horse because she had been thinking about it before he interrupted and she spoke of it timidly, but it was only an excuse to say something.

"You can't catch it," he said, shaking his head.

Here the neighbor broke in: "It's easy enough to catch it; this last week three children have stroked it—it's pretty low, I guess; but I doubt if it would be able to walk that far."

He looked over the rim of the teacup to see how this remark would be taken—he felt excited all of a sudden at the thought that something was going to be attempted that had not been attempted in many years, and a feeling of misfortune took hold of him that he had certainly not felt at Pauvla Agrippa's death. Everything about the place, and his life that had seemed to him quite normal and natural, now seemed strange.

The disrupting of one idea—that the horse could not be caught—put him into a mood that made all other accustomed things alien.

However, after this it seemed quite natural that they should make the effort and Tasha went into the room where Pauvla Agrippa lay.

The boy had fallen asleep in the corner and Pauvla's baby was crawling over him, making for Pauvla, cooing softly and saying "mamma" with difficulty, because the little under lip kept reaching to the upper lip to prevent the saliva from interrupting the call.

Tasha put her foot in the baby's way and stood looking down at Pauvla Agrippa, where her small hands lay beneath her fine breast with its purple veins, and now Tasha did not feel quite the same resentment that she had felt earlier. It is true this body had done something irrevocable to Pauvla Agrippa, but she also realized that she, Tasha, must now do something to this body; it was the same with everything, nothing was left as it was, something was always altering something else. Perhaps it was an unrecognized law.

Pauvla Agrippa's husband had gone out to see what could be done with the mare, and now the neighbor came in, saying that it would not come in over the sand, but that he—the husband—thought that it would walk toward the headland, as it was wont.

"If you could only carry her out to it," he said.

Tasha called in two of her brothers and woke up the one on the floor. "Everything will be arranged for her comfort," she said, "when we get her up there." They lifted Pauvla Agrippa up and her baby began to laugh, asking to be lifted up also, and holding its little hands high that it might be lifted, but no one was paying any attention to him, because now they were moving his mother.

Pauvla Agrippa looked fine as they carried her, only her small hands parted and deserted the cleft where they had lain, dropping down upon the shoulders of her brothers. Several children stood hand in hand watching, and one or two villagers appeared who had heard from the neighbors what was going on.

The mare had been induced to stand and someone had slipped a halter over its neck for the first time in many years; there was a frightened look in the one eye and the film that covered the other seemed to darken, but it made no objection when they raised Pauvla Agrippa and placed her on its back, tying her on with a fish net.

Then someone laughed, and the neighbor slapped his leg saying, "Look what the old horse has come to—caught and burdened at last." And he watched the mare with small cruel eyes.

Pauvla Agrippa's husband took the strap of the halter and began plodding through the sand, the two boys on either side of the horse holding to all that was left of Pauvla Agrippa. Tasha came behind, her hands folded, praying now to this horse, still trying to find peace, but she noticed with a little apprehension that the horse's flanks had begun to quiver, and that this quiver was extending to its ribs and from its ribs to its forelegs.

Then she saw it turn a little, lifting its head. She called out to Pauvla Agrippa's husband who, startled with the movement and the cry, dropped the rope.

The mare had turned toward the sea; for an instant it stood there, quivering, a great thin bony thing with crooked legs; its blind eyes half covered with the black coarse lashes. Pauvla Agrippa with her head thrown a bit back rested easily, it seemed, the plaits of her yellow hair lying about her neck, but away from her face, because she was not supported quite right; still she looked like some strange new sea animal beneath the net that held her from falling.

Then without warning, no-man's-mare jumped forward and plunged neck-deep into the water.

A great wave came up, covered it, receded, and it could be seen swimming, its head out of the water, while Pauvla Agrippa's loosened yellow hair floated behind. No one moved. Another wave rose high, descended, and again the horse was seen swimming with head up, and this time Pauvla's Agrippa's hands were parted and lay along the water as though she were swimming.

The most superstitious among them began crossing themselves, and one woman dropped on her knees, rocking from side to side; and still no one moved.

And this time the wave rose, broke and passed on, leaving the surface smooth.

That night Tasha picked up Pauvla Agrippa's sleepy boy and standing in the doorway prayed to the sea, and this time she found comfort.

OSCAR

Before the house rose two stately pine trees, and all about small firs and hemlocks. The garden path struggled up to the porch between wildflowers and weeds, and looming against its ancient bulk the shadows of out-houses and barns.

It stood among the hills, and just below around a curve in the road, lay the placid gray reservoir.

Sometimes parties would cross the fields, walking slowly toward the mountains. And sometimes children could be heard murmuring in the underbrush of things they scarcely knew.

Strange things had happened in this country town. Murder, theft, and little girls found weeping, and silent morose boys scowling along in the ragweed, with half-shut sunburned eyelids.

The place was wild, deserted and impossible in winter. In summer it was overrun with artists and town folk with wives and babies. Every Saturday there were fairs on the green, where second-hand articles were sold for a song, and flirting was formidable and passing. There were picnics, mountain climbing, speeches in the town hall, on the mark of the beast, on sin, and democracy, and once in a while a lecture on something that "everyone should know," attended by mothers, their offspring left with servants who knew what everyone shouldn't.

Then there were movies, bare legs, deacons, misses in cascades of curls and on Sunday one could listen to Mr. Widdie, the clergyman, who suffered from consumption, speak on love of one's neighbor.

In this house and in this town had lived, for some fifteen years or so, Emma Gonsberg.

She was a little creature, lively, smiling, extremely good-natured. She had been married twice, divorced once, and was now a widow still in her thirties.

Of her two husbands she seldom said anything. Once she made the remark: "Only fancy, they never did catch on to me at all."

She tried to be fashionable, did her hair in the Venetian style, wore gowns after the manner of Lady de Bath entering her carriage; and tried to cultivate only those who could tell her "where she stood."

Her son Oscar was fourteen or thereabouts. He wore distinctly over-decorative English clothes, and remembered two words of some obscure Indian dialect that seemed to mean "fleas," for whenever he flung these words defiantly at visitors, they would go off into peals of laughter, headed by his mother. At such times he would lower his eyes and show a row of too heavy teeth.

Emma Gonsberg loved flowers but could not grow them. She admired cats because there was "nothing servile about them," but they would not stay with her; and though she loved horses and longed to be one of those daring women who could handle them "without being crushed in the stalls," they nevertheless ignored her with calm indifference. Of her loves, passions and efforts, she had managed to raise a few ill-smelling pheasants, and had to let it go at that.

In the winter she led a lonely and discriminating life. In the summer her house filled with mixed characters, as one might say. A hot melancholy Jew, an officer who was always upon the point of depreciating his medals in a conceited voice, and one other who swore inoffensively.

Finally, she had given this sort of thing up, partly because she had managed, soon after, to get herself entangled with a man called Ulric Straussmann. A tall rough fellow, who said he came from the Tyrol; a fellow without sensibilities but with a certain bitter sensuality. A good-natured creature as far as he went, with vivid streaks of German lust, which had at once something sentimental and something careless about it; the type who can turn the country, with a single gesture, into a brothel, and makes of children strong enemies. He showed no little audacity in putting things into people's minds that he would not do himself.

He smelled very strongly of horses and was proud of it. He pretended a fondness for all that goes under hide or hair, but a collie bitch, known for her gentleness, snapped at him and bit him. He invariably carried a leather thong, braided at the base for a handle, and would stand for hours talking, with his legs apart, whirling this contrived whip, and, looking out of the corner of his eyes, would pull his mustache, waiting to see which of the ladies would draw her feet in.

He talked in a rather even, slightly nasal tone, wetting his lips with a long out-thrust of tongue, like an animal. His teeth were splendid and his tongue unusually red, and he prided himself on these and on the calves of his legs. They were large, muscular and rather handsome.

He liked to boast that there was nothing that he could not do and be forgiven, because, as he expressed it, "I have always left people satisfied." If it were hate or if it were love, he seemed to have come off with unusual success. "Most people are puny," he would add, "while I am large, strong, healthy. Solid flesh through and through," whereat he would pound his chest and smile.

He was new to the town and sufficiently insolent to attract attention. There was also something childishly naive in him, as there is in all tall and robust men who talk about themselves. This probably saved him, because when he was drinking, he often became gross and insulting, but he soon put the women of the party in a good humor by giving one of them a hearty and good-natured slap on the rear that she was not likely to forget.

Besides this man, Emma had a few old friends of the less interesting, though better-read, type. Among them, however, was an exception, Oliver Kahn, a married man with several children one heard of and never saw. A strange, quiet man who was always talking. He had splendid eyes and a poor mouth—very full lips. In the beginning one surmised that he had been quite an adventurer. He had an odor about him of the rather recent cult of the "terribly good." He seemed to have been unkind to his family in some way and was spending the rest of his life in a passion of regret and remorse. He had become one of those guests who are only missed when absent. He finally stayed for good, sleeping in an ante-room with his boots on—his one royal habit.

In the beginning Emma had liked him tremendously. He was at once gentle and furious, but of late, just prior to the Straussmann affair, he had begun to irritate her. She thought to herself, "He is going mad, that's all." She was angry at herself for saying "that's all," as if she had expected something different, more momentous.

He had enormous appetites, he ate like a Porthos and drank like a Pantagruel, and talked hour after hour about the same thing, "Love of one's neighbor," and spent his spare time in standing with his hands behind him, in front of the pheasants' cage. He had been a snipe hunter in his time, and once went on a big game hunt, but now he said he saw something more significant here.

He had, like all good sportsmen, even shot himself through the hand, but of late he pretended that he did not remember what the scar came from.

He seemed to suffer a good deal. Evil went deep and good went deep and he suffered the tortures of the damned. He wept and laughed and ate and drank and slept, and year by year his eyes grew sweeter, tenderer, and his mouth fuller, more gross.

The child Oscar did not like Kahn, yet sometimes he would become extraordinarily excited, talk very fast, almost banteringly, a little malignly, and once when Kahn had taken his hand, he drew it away angrily. "Don't," he said.

"Why not?"

"Because it is dirty," he retorted maliciously.

"As if you really knew of what I was thinking," Kahn said, and put his own hands behind him.

Emma liked Kahn, was attached to him. He mentioned her faults without regret or reproval, and this in itself was a divine sort of love.

He would remark: "We cannot be just because we are bewildered; we ought to be proud enough to welcome our enemies as judges, but we hate, and to hate is the act of the incurious. I love with an everlasting but a changing love, because I know I am the wrong sort of man to be good—and because I revere the shadow on the threshold."

"What shadow, Kahn?"

"In one man we called it Christ—it is energy; for most of us it is dead, a phantom. If you have it you are Christ, and if you have only a little of it you are but the promise of the Messiah."

These seemed great words, and she looked at him with a little admiring smile.

"You make me uneasy for fear that I have not said 'I love you with an everlasting love,' often enough to make it an act of fanaticism."

As for Oscar, he did what he liked, which gave him character, but made him difficult to live with.

He was not one of those "weedy" youths, long of leg, and stringy like "jerked beef, thank God!" as his mother said to visitors. He was rather too full-grown, thick of calf and hip and rather heavy of feature. His hands and feet were not out of proportion as is usually the case with children of his age, but they were too old looking.

He did not smoke surreptitiously. On the contrary he had taken out a pipe one day in front of his mother, and filling it, smoked in silence, not even with a frightened air, and for that matter not even with a particularly bold air;—he did it quite simply, as something he had finally decided to do, and Emma Gonsberg had gone off to Kahn with it, in a rather helpless manner.

Most children swing in circles about a room, clumsily. Oscar on the contrary walked into the four corners placidly and officially, looked at the back of the books here and a picture there, and even grunted approvingly at one or two in quite a mature manner.

He had a sweetheart, and about her and his treatment of her there were only a few of the usual signs—he was shy, and passionately immersed in her, there was little of the casual smartness of first calf love about it, though he did in truth wave her off with a grin if he was questioned.

He took himself with seriousness amounting to a lack of humor—and though he himself knew that he was a youth, and had the earmarks of adolescence about him—and know it he certainly did—once he said, "Well, what of it—is that any reason why I should not be serious about everything?" This remark had so astonished his mother that she had immediately sent for Kahn to know if he thought the child was precocious—and Kahn had answered, "If he were, I should be better pleased."

"But what is one to expect?"

"Children," he answered, "are never what they are supposed to be, and they never have been. He may be old for his age, but what child hasn't been?"

In the meantime, she tried to bring Straussmann and Kahn together—"My house is all at odds," she thought, but these two never hit it off. Straussmann always appeared dreadfully superficial and cynical, and Kahn dull and good about nothing.

"They have both got abnormal appetites," she thought wearily. She listened to them trying to talk together of an evening on the piazza steps. Kahn was saying:

"You must, however, warn yourself, in fact I might say arm yourself, against any sensation of pleasure in doing good; this is very difficult, I know, but it can be attained. You can give and forgive and tolerate gently and, as one might say, casually, until it's a second nature."

"There you have it, tolerate—who wants tolerance, or a second nature? Well, let us drop it. I feel like a child—it's difficult not to feel like a child."

"Like Oscar—he has transports—even at his age," Emma added hesitatingly. "Perhaps that's not quite as it should be?"

"The memory of growing up is worse than the fear of death," Kahn remarked, and Emma sighed.

"I don't know; the country was made for children, they say—I could tell you a story about that," Straussmann broke off, whistling to Oscar. "Shall I tell Oscar about the country—and what it is really like?" he asked Emma, turning his head.

"Let the boy alone."

"Why, over there in that small village," Straussmann went on, taking Oscar by the arm. "It is a pretty tale I could tell you—perhaps I will when you are older—but don't let your mother persuade you that the country is a nice, healthful, clean place, because, my child, it's corrupt."

"Will you let the boy alone!" Emma cried, turning very red.

"Ah, eh—I'll let him alone right enough—but it won't make much difference you'll see," he went on. "There is a great deal told to children that they should not hear, I'll admit, but there wasn't a thing I didn't know when I was ten. It happened one day in a hotel in Southampton—a dark place, gloomy, smelling frightfully of mildew, the walls were damp and stained. A strange place, eh, to learn the delights of love, but then our parents seldom dwell on the delights—they are too taken up with the sordid details, the mere sordid details. My father had a great beard, and I remember thinking that it would have been better if he hadn't said such things. I wasn't much good afterwards for five or six years, but my sister was different. She enjoyed it immensely and forgot all about it almost immediately, excepting when I reminded her."

"Go to bed, Oscar," Emma said abruptly.

He went, and on going up the steps he did not let his fingers trail along the spindles of the banisters with his usual "Eeny meeny miny mo," etc.

Emma was a little troubled and watched him going up silently, hardly moving his arms.

"Children should be treated very carefully, they should know as much as possible, but in a less superficial form than they must know later."

"I think a child is born corrupt and attains to decency," Straussmann said grinning.

"If you please," Emma cried gaily, "we will talk about things we understand."

Kahn smiled. "It's beautiful, really beautiful," he said, meaning her gaiety. He always said complimentary things about her lightness of spirit, and always in an angry voice.

"Come, come, you are going mad. What's the good of that?" she said, abruptly, thinking, "He is a man who discovered himself once too often."

"You are wrong, Emma, I am not worthy of madness."

"Don't be on your guard, Kahn," she retorted.

Oscar appeared before her suddenly, barefoot.

She stared at him. "What is it?" she at last managed to ask in a faint almost suffocated voice.

"I want to kiss you," he whispered.

She moved toward him slowly, when, halfway, he hurried toward her, seized her hand, kissed it, and went back into the house.

"My God," she cried out. "He is beginning to think for himself," and ran in after him.

She remembered how she had talked to him the night before, only the night before. "You must love with an everlasting but a changing love," and he became restless. "With an everlasting but a changing love."

"What do you mean by 'changing'?" His palms were moist, and his feet twitched.

"A love that takes in every detail, every element—that can understand without hating, without distinction, I think."

"Why do you say, 'I think'?"

"I mean, I know," she answered, confused.

"Get that Kahn out, he's a rascal," he said, abruptly, grinning.

"What are you saying, Oscar?" she demanded, turning cold. "I'll never come to your bed again, take your hands and say, 'Our Father.'"

"It will be all right if you send that man packing," he said, stressing the word "packing."

She was very angry, and half started toward the door. Then she turned back. "Why do you say that, Oscar?"

"Because he makes you nervous—well, then—because he crouches"; he saw by his mother's face that she was annoyed, puzzled, and he turned red to his ears. "I don't mean that, I mean he isn't good; he's just watching for something good to happen, to take place—" His voice trailed off, and he raised his eyes solemn and full of tears to her face. She leaned down and kissed him, tucking him in like a "little boy."

"But I'm not a little boy," he called out to her.

And tonight, she did not come down until she thought Kahn and Straussmann had gone.

Kahn had disappeared, but Straussmann had taken a turn or two about the place and was standing in the shadow of the stoop when she came out.

"Come," he said. "What is it that you want?"

"I think it's religion," she answered abruptly. "But it's probably love."

"Let us take a walk," he suggested.

They turned in toward the shadows of the great still mountains and the denser, more arrogant shadows of the outhouses and barns. She looked away into the silence, and the night, and a warm sensation as of pleasure or of something expected but intangible came over her, and she wanted to laugh, to cry, and thinking of it she knew that it was neither.

She was almost unconscious of him for a little, thinking of her son. She raised her long silk skirts about her ankles and tramped off into the dampness. A whippoorwill was whistling off to the right. It sounded as if he were on the fence, and Emma stopped and tried to make it out. She took Ulric's arm presently, and feeling his muscles swell began to think of the Bible. "Those who take by the sword shall die by the sword. And those who live by the flesh shall die by the flesh."

She wished that she had someone she could believe in. She saw a door before her mental eye, and herself opening it and saying, "Now tell me this, and what it means—only today I was thinking 'those who live by the flesh'"—and as suddenly the door was slammed in her face. She started back.

"You are nervous," he said in a pleased whisper.

Heavy stagnant shadows sprawled in the path. "So many million leaves and twigs to make one dark shadow," she said, and was sorry because it sounded childishly romantic, quite different from what she had intended, what she had meant.

They turned the corner of the carriage-house.

Something moved, a toad, gray and ugly, bounced across her feet and into the darkness of the hedges. Coming to the entrance of the barn they paused. They could distinguish sleeping hens, the white films moving on their eyes—and through a window at the back, steam rising from the dung heap.

"There don't seem to be any real farmers left," she said aloud, thinking of some book she had read about the troubles of the peasants and landholders.

"You're thinking of my country," he said smiling.

"No, I wasn't," she said. "I was wondering what it is about the country that makes it seem so terrible?"

"It's your being a Puritan—a tight-laced delightful little Puritan."

She winced at the words and decided to remain silent.

It was true, Straussmann was in a fever of excitement—he was always this way with women, especially with Emma. He tried to conceal it for the time being, thinking, rightly, that a display of it would not please her just at the moment—"but it would be only a matter of minutes when she would welcome it," he promised himself, and waited.

He reflected that she would laugh at him. "But she would enjoy it just the same. The way with all women who have had anything to do with more than one man and are not yet forty," he reflected. "They like what they get, but they laugh at you, and know you are lying—"

"Oh, my God!" Emma said suddenly, drawing her arm away and wiping her face with her handkerchief.

"What's the matter?"

"Nothing, it's the heat."

"It is warm," he said dismally.

"I despise everything, I really despise everything, but you won't believe—I mean everything when I say everything—you'll think I mean some one thing—won't you?" she went on hurriedly. She felt that she was becoming hysterical.

"It doesn't matter," he rejoined, walking on beside her, his heart beating violently. "Down, you dog," he said aloud.

"What is that?" She raised her eyes and he looked into them, and they both smiled.

"That's better. I wish I were God."

"A desire for a vocation."

"Not true, and horrid, as usual," she answered, and she was hot and angry all at once.

He pulled at his mustache and sniffed. "I can smell the hedges—ah, the country is a gay deceiver—it smells pleasant enough, but it's treacherous. The country, my dear Emma, has done more to corrupt man, to drag him down, to turn him loose upon his lower instincts, than morphine, alcohol and women. That's why I like it, that's why it's the perfect place for women. They are devils and should be driven out, and as there's more room in the country and consequently less likelihood of driving them out in too much of a hurry, there is more time for amusement." He watched her out of the corner of his eye as he said these things to note if they were ill advised. They seemed to leave her cold, but tense.

A little later they passed the barns again.

"What was that?" Emma asked suddenly.

"I heard nothing."

But she had heard something, and her heart beat fearfully. She recognized Oscar's voice. She reached up, signing Straussmann to be quiet. She did not want him to hear; she wished that the ground would yawn, would swallow him up.

"See that yellow flower down there," she said, pointing toward the end of the path they had just come. "I want it, I must have it, please." He did as he was bid, amiably enough.

She listened—she heard the voice of Oscar's little sweetheart: "It seems as if we were one already . . ." It was high, resolute, unflagging, without emotion, a childish parroting of some novel. Oscar's voice came back, half smothered:

"Do you really care—more than you like Berkeley?"

"Yes, I do," she answered in the same false treble, "lots more."

"Come here," he said softly—the hay rustled.

"I don't want to—the rye gets into my hair and spoils it."

"Dolly, do you like the country?"

"Yes, I do"—without conviction.

"We will go to the city," he answered.

"Oh, Oscar, you're so strong," she giggled, and it sent a cold shudder through Emma's being.

Then presently, "What's the matter, Oscar—why, you're crying."

"I'm not—well, then yes, I am—what of it?—you'll understand, too, some day."

She was evidently frightened, because she said in a somewhat loosened key, "No one would ever believe that we were as much in love as we are, would they, Oscar?"

"No, why do you ask that?"

"It's a great pity," she said again with the false sound, and sighed.

"Do you care? Why do you care?"

Straussmann was coming back with the yellow flower between thumb and forefinger. Emma ran a little way to meet him.

"Come, let us go home the other way."

"Rather, let us not go home," he said, boldly, and took her wrist, hurting her.

"Ah," she said. "Vous m'avez blessée d'amour"—ironically.

"Yes, speak French, it helps women like you at such moments," he said, brutally, and kissed her.

But kissing him back, she thought, "The fool, why does Oscar take her so seriously when they are both children, and she is torturing him?"

"My love, my sweet, my little love," he was babbling.

She tried to quench this, trembling a little. "But tell me, my friend—no, not so hasty—what do you think of immortality?" He had pushed her so far back that there was no regaining her composure. "My God, in other words, what of the will to retribution!"

But she could not go on. "I've tried to," she thought.

Later, when the dawn was almost upon them, he said: "How sad to be drunk, only to die. For the end of all man is Fate, in other words, the end of all man is vulgar."

She felt the need of something that had not been.

"I'm not God, you see, after all."

"So I see, madam," he said. "But you're a damned clever little woman."

When she came in, she found Kahn lying flat on his back, his eyes wide open.

"Couldn't you sleep?"

"No, I could not sleep."

She was angry. "I'm sorry—you suffer."

"Yes, a little."

"Kahn," she cried in anguish, flinging herself on her knees beside him. "What should I have done, what shall I do?"

He put his hand on her cheek. "My dear, my dear," he said, and sighed. "I perhaps was wrong."

She listened.

"Very wrong, I see it all now; I am an evil man, an old and an evil being."

"No, no!"

"Yes, yes," he said gently, softly, contradicting her. "Yes, evil, and pitiful, and weak"; he seemed to be trying to remember something. "What is it that I have overlooked?" He asked the question in such a confused voice that she was startled.

"Is it hate?" she asked.

"I guess so, yes, I guess that's it."

"Kahn, try to think—there must be something else."

"Madness."

She began to shiver.

"Are you cold?"

"No, it's not cold."

"No, it's not cold," he repeated after her. "You are not cold, Emma, you are a child."

Tears began to roll down her cheeks.

"Yes," he continued sadly. "You too will hear: remorse is the medium through which the evil spirit takes possession."

And again, he cried out in anguish. "But I'm *not* superficial—I may have been wanton, but I've not been superficial. I wanted to give up everything, to abandon myself to whatever IT demanded, to do whatever IT directed and willed. But the terrible thing is I don't know what abandon is. I don't know when it's abandon and when it's just a case of minor calculation.

"The real abandon is not to know whether one throws oneself off a cliff or not, and not to care. But I can't do it, because I must know, because I'm afraid if I did cast myself off, I should find that I had thrown myself off the lesser thing after all, and that," he said in a horrified voice, "I could never outlive, I could never have faith again. And so it is that I shall never know, Emma; only children and the naive know, and I am too sophisticated to accomplish the divine descent."

"But you must tell me," she said, hurriedly. "What am I to do, what am I to think? My whole future depends on that, on your answer—on knowing whether I do an injustice not to hate, not to strike, not to kill—well, you must tell me—I swear it is my life—my entire life."

"Don't ask me, I can't know, I can't tell. I who could not lead one small sheep, what could I do with a soul, and what still more could I do with you? No," he continued, "I'm so incapable. I am so mystified. Death would be a release, but it wouldn't settle anything. It never settles anything, it simply wipes the slate, it's merely a way of putting the sum out of mind, yet I wish I might die. How do I know now but that everything I have thought, and said, and done, has not been false, a little abyss from which I shall crawl laughing at the evil of my own limitation."

"But the child—what have I been telling Oscar—to love with an everlasting love—"

"That's true," he said.

"Kahn, listen. What have I done to him, what have I done to myself? What are we all doing here—are we all mad—or are we merely excited—overwrought, hysterical? I must know, I must know." She took his hand, and he felt her tears upon it.

"Kahn, is it an everlasting but a changing love—what kind of love is that?"

"Perhaps that's it," he cried, jumping up, and with a gesture tore his shirt open at the throat. "Look, I want you to see, I run upon the world with a bared breast—but never find the blade—ah, the civility of our own damnation—that's the horror. A few years ago, surely this could not have happened. Do you know," he said, turning his eyes all hot and burning upon her, "the most terrible thing in the world is to bare the breast and never to feel the blade enter!" He buried his face in his hands.

"But, Kahn, you must think, you must give me an answer. All this indecision is all very well for us, for all of us who are too old to change, for all of us who can reach God through some plaything we have used as a symbol, but there's my son, what is he to think, to feel, he has no jester's stick to shake, nor stool to stand on. Am I responsible for him? Why," she cried frantically, "must I be responsible for him? I tell you I won't be, I can't. I won't take it upon myself. But I have, I have. Is there something that can make me immune to my own blood? Tell me—I must wipe the slate—the fingers are driving me mad—can't he stand alone now? Oh, Kahn, Kahn!" she cried, kissing his hands. "See, I kiss your hands, I am doing so much. You must be the prophet—you can't do less for the sign I give you—I must know, I must receive an answer, I will receive it."

He shook her off suddenly, a look of fear came into his eyes.

"Are you trying to frighten me?" he whispered. She went into the hall, into the dark, and did not know why, or understand anything. Her mind was on fire, and it was consuming things that were strange and merciful and precious.

Finally, she went into her son's room and stood before his bed. He lay with one feverish cheek against a dirty hand, his knees drawn up; his mouth had a peculiar look of surprise about it.

She bent down, called to him, not knowing what she was doing. "Wrong, wrong," she whispered, and she shook him by the shoulders. "Listen, Oscar, get up. Listen to me!"

He awoke and cried out as one of her tears, forgotten, cold, struck against his cheek. An ague shook his limbs. She brought her face close to his.

"Son, hate too, that is inevitable—irrevocable—"

He put out his two hands and pushed them against her breast and in a subdued voice said, "Go away, go away," and he looked as if he were about to cry, but he did not cry.

She turned and fled into the hall.

However, in the morning, at breakfast, there was nothing unusual about her, but a tired softness and yielding of spirit; and at dinner, which was always late, she felt only a weary indifference when she saw Straussmann coming up the walk. He had a red and white handkerchief about his throat, and she thought, "How comic he looks."

"Good evening," he said.

"Good evening," she answered, and a touch of her old gaiety came into her voice. Kahn was already seated, and now she motioned Straussmann to follow. She began slicing the cold potted beef and asked them about sugar in their tea, adding, "Oscar will be here soon." To Kahn she showed only a very little trace of coldness, of indecision.

"No," Straussmann said, still standing, legs apart: "If you'll excuse me, I'd like a word or two with Kahn." They stepped off the porch together.

"Kahn," he said, going directly to the point, "listen." He took hold of Kahn's coat by the lapel. "You have known Emma longer than I have; you've got to break it to her." He flourished a large key under Kahn's nose, as he spoke.

"I've got him locked up in the outhouse safe enough for the present, but we must do something immediately."

"What's the matter?" A strange, pleasant but cold sweat broke out upon Kahn's forehead.

"I found Oscar sitting beside the body of his sweetheart, what's-her-name; he had cut her throat with a kitchen knife, yes, with a kitchen knife—he seemed calm, but he would say nothing. What shall we do?"

"They'll say he was a degenerate from the start—"

"Those who live by the flesh—eh?"

"No," Kahn said, in a confused voice, "that's not it."

They stood and stared at each other so long that presently Emma grew nervous and came down the garden path to hear what it was all about.

THE RABBIT

The road had been covered with leaves on the day that the little tailor had left his own land. He said good day and good-bye in the one breath, with his broad teeth apart as if he had been hauled out of deep water. He did not leave Armenia because he wanted to, he left because he had to. There wasn't a thing about Armenia that he did not want to stay with for ever; it was necessity, he was being pushed out. In short, he had been left a property in New York City.

Leave-taking did not tear him to pieces, he wept no tears, the falling leaves sent no pang through him, he treated the whole business as a simple and resigned man should. He let Armenia slip through his fingers.

His life had been a sturdy, steady, slow, pleasant sort of thing. He ploughed and tended his crops. Hands folded over the haft of his scythe, he watched his cow grazing. He groomed the feathers and beaks of his ducks to see that the feathers lay straight, the bills unbroken and shining. He liked to pass his hands over the creatures of his small land, they were exactly as pleasing as plants; in fact, he could not see much difference, when you came right down to it.

Now it was otherwise. His people advised him (as he was a single man) to accept his inheritance, a small tailoring business his uncle had left him. With a helper, they said, it might be the very best thing for him. It might "educate" him, make him into an "executive," a "boss," a man of the world.

He protested, but not with any great force; he was a timid man, a gentle man. He cleaned the spade, sharpened the saws, shook the shavings out of the plane, oiled his auger and bit, rubbed fat into the harness, and pulling his last calf from the drenched and murmuring cow, wondered what to do.

The day he was to leave he went first into the forest where he had brought boughs down, tying them, to make a hut against the sun. His jug of molasses and cinnamon water was still there by his sitting log. The woods spilled over into the road; the shadows, torn through with bright holes of sunlight, danced in patches of bloom. Mosquitoes from the swamp sang about his head. They got into the long hairs of his beard below his chin, and clung, whining in the mesh, wheeled against his cheek, flying up above his clashing hands, and as he slapped his face, he thought of himself sitting in quiet misfortune, sewing, up on a table, as though he had died and had to work it out.

So one day, to the lower part of Manhattan (to the street of the shop of Amietiev the tailor) came a stranger, the latest Amietiev, with a broom. The passers-by saw him swinging it over the boards of his inheritance, a room not much more than twelve by twenty-four, the back third curtained off, to hide the small bed and the commode beside it. He tested the air, as he had tested the air of his country, he sneezed; he held the room up in his eye by the scruff of its neck, as you might say, and shook it in the face of his lost acres.

He had learned the tailors' trade when he was a young boy, when this now dead uncle had been his guardian, but his fingers were clumsy and he broke the needle. He worked slowly and painfully, holding his breath too long, puffing it out in loud sighs. He toiled far into the night, the goose between his knees. People on the way home peered in at him as he sat on his table-top, half hidden by the signs in his windows, the fly-specked fashion book open at the swaggering gentlemen in topcoats; out-of-date announcements of religious meetings, and bills for the local burlesque. Loiterers, noting how pale he was, remarked to each other, "That one will die of the consumption, see if he doesn't!"

Across the way, laid out on a butcher's slab (vying with Armietiev's remnants of silk linings, shepherd checks and woolen stuffs), were bright quarters of beef, calves' heads and knuckle bones; remnants of animals, pink and yellow layers of fat. There were muscle meats and kidneys, with their webbings of suet; great carcasses, slashed down the center showing the keyboard of the spine, and hanging on hooks, ducks dripping, head down, into basins.

When the little tailor looked up, it made him horribly sad; the colors were a very harvest of death. He remembered too easily the swinging meadows of his own country, with the cows in the lanes and the fruits overhead, and he turned away and went on stitching.

Behind the curtain was a small gas-ring on which he warmed his breakfast; sometimes a sausage, always coffee, bread, cheese. In the summer it was too hot, in the winter the shop was deadly with heavy air; he could not risk opening the door. He was flooded with chill whenever a customer came in (no one ever seemed to think he might feel the wind); so he sat in the foul air, made infinitely worse by the gas stove, and day by day his eyes grew farther back in his head, the dark brows more and more prominent. The children of the neighborhood called him "coal eye."

In the second summer business picked up, he worked more quickly, did excellent patchwork, charged very little and never gave himself any time for his own life at all; he stitched, turned, pressed, altered, as though the world were a huge barricade of old clothes. At about this time he had become attached to a small, ill, slender Italian girl, who had first appeared carrying her father's coat. She smelled tart, as of lemons.

Her straight black hair, parted in the middle, was as black as her eyes; under a dipping nose blazed her mouth, firm, shut. Almost anything bright caught at him. He thought of all the calendars with all the Madonnas that he had seen, and he made the mistake of shuffling this girl in with them. The sharp, avaricious cruelty of her face pleased him; he confused the quick darting head with brightness. He himself was not a good-looking man; this did not trouble him, he was as good-looking as anyone in his family and that was that. He was quite unconscious that for the size of his head, his body was rather small; the fact that he had coarse hair made matters worse.

This girl, Addie, mentioned all these things. It hurt him because he was beginning to like her. He noticed that when he showed it, by the trembling of his needle, she laughed and looked starved. He was puzzled. "Why," he asked, "when you say such things about me, do you look so pretty?"

This being the very worst thing he could say, it encouraged her, it flattered her. She throve on whetting, and he was always putting an edge on her: after all, she was neither as nice as he thought, nor as young. Finally, after much debate with himself, with slow tortuous convulsions of mind, he asked her if she had thought of love and marriage. Of course she had; here was a business right there before her for the taking, it was promising and seemed to be going to "flourish" as you might put it, and wasn't she already used to him? In a quiet, canny, measured way (that he was much too much of an idiot to notice) she had made her plans. She was pleased to admit the attachment, but what she said was, "You are a poor sort of man!" She said it roughly (as if blaming him for something). She said it bridling, pulling her pleated skirt between two fingers in a straight line. He felt that she was very stout; himself, very nothing.

"What do you want that I shall do?"

She shrugged, flipped her hair back, opened her entire mouth, exposing the full length of the crouching tongue.

"I mean, if I must do something, what is it? If as you say, I am only—"

"You'll never *be* anything," she said, then she added, "You'll never be anything *else*."

"True, not something else, but perhaps more?"

"Now there's a likely." She had a way of clipping her meanings short, it was her form of scorn.

"What do you mean by 'a *likely*'?"

"You are not the sort, for instance . . ."

"For?" He turned his body, looking at her closely.

"You are hardly a *hero*!" She laughed in a series of short snapping sounds, like a dog.

"Are heroes the style?" he asked, with such utter guile and with such a troubled face that she tittered.

"Not in your family, I take it."

He nodded. "That is true, yes, that is quite true. We were quiet people. You do not like quiet people?"

"Foo!" she said, "they are women!"

He pondered this a long time. Slowly he got off his table; he took her by both shoulders, shaking her softly from side to side.

"That is not true and you know it; they are something else."

She began shouting, "*So*, now I'm a liar. This is what it has come to! I'm abominable, unnatural, unnatural!" She had managed to get herself into the highest sort of pretended indignation, pulling her hair, swinging it like a whip from side to side. In so laying hold on herself, in disarranging her usually composed, almost casual ease, the sly baggage had him in as great a state of distress, as if he had had to witness the shaking of an holy image.

"No, no!" he cried, clapping his hands together. "Don't do it, leave yourself alone! I'll do something, I'll make everything as it should be." He came to her, drawing her hair out of her fist. "For you I will do *anything*. Yes, surely, I will do it, I will, I will!"

"You will do *what*, Amietiev?" she asked, with such sudden calm that his anxiety almost stumbled over her. "What is it that you will do?"

"I shall be less like a woman. You called me a woman; a terrible thing to say to a man, especially if he is small, and I am small."

She came forward, her elbows tight to her sides, her palms out, walking sideways: "You'll do anything for me? What? Something daring, something really *big*, something grand, just for me?"

"Just for you." He looked at her in sorrow. The cruel passing twist of the mouth—(everything about her was fleeting)—the perishing thin arms, the small cage of the ribs, the too long hair, the hands turning on the wrists, the sliding narrow feet, and the faint mournful sharp odor of lemons that puffed from her swinging skirt, moved him away from her; grief in all his being, snuffed him out. She came up behind him, caught both his hands, pulling them backward, and leaning against him, kissed him on the neck. He tried to turn around, but she held him; so they stood for a moment, then she broke away and ran out into the street.

He set to work again, sitting cross-legged on the table. He wondered what he was supposed to do. Nothing like this had happened before; in fact, he had always told her how he longed for a country life, with her beside him in the fields, or sitting among the plants and vegetables. Now here he was faced with himself as a hero . . . what was a hero? What was the difference between himself and that sort of man? He tried to think if he had ever known one. He remembered tales told him by the gypsies, a great time ago, when he was in his own land; they had certainly told him of a lad who was a tremendous fighter, who wrestled with his adversary like a demon, but at the end, not being able to kill anything, had thrown himself off a mountain. But for himself, a tailor, such a thing would be impossible . . . he would only die and that would not get him anywhere. He thought of all the great people he had read of, or heard of, or might have brushed against. There was Jean the blacksmith, who had lost an eye saving his child from a horse; but if he, Amietiev, lost an eye, Addie would not like him at all. How about Napoleon? There was a well-known man; he had done everything, all by himself, more or less, so much so that he even crowned himself Emperor without any help at all, and people so admired him they hung his picture all over the world, because of course he had been such a master at killing. He thought about this a long time, and finally came to the inevitable conclusion: all heroes were men who killed or got killed.

Well, that was impossible; if he were killed, he might as well have stayed in the country and never laid eyes on Addie—therefore he must kill—but what?

He might of course save someone or something, but there would have to be danger of one kind or another, and there might not be any for days and days, and he was tired and afraid of waiting.

He laid his work aside, slid off the table, lowered the light, and lying face down on his cot, tried to think the whole thing out.

He sat up, rubbing both hands on the sides of his face; it was damp under the beard, he could feel it. He tried to make a picture for his mind, a picture of what killing was like. He sat on the edge of the cot, staring at the small piece of carpet with its Persian design, his mind twisted in it.

He thought of trees, the brook where he went fishing, the green fields, the cows who breathed a long band of hot air from their nostrils when he came close; he thought of the geese, he thought of thin ice on the ponds with bushes bristling out of it . . . he thought of Addie, and Addie was entwined with the idea of killing. He tried to think of himself as of someone destroying someone. He clapped his palms together, lacing the fingers in a lock. No, no, no! That wouldn't press out the life of a thrush. He held his hands apart, looking at the thumbs. He rubbed them down the sides of his legs. What a terrible thing murder was! He stood up, shaking his body from side to side, as if it hurt him. He went out into the shop, pulling up the shade as high as it would go.

Exactly opposite, two bright lights burned in the butcher's window. He could see sides of beef hanging from their hooks, the chilled lakes of blood in the platters, the closed eyes of the calves' heads in ranks on their slabs, looking like peeled women, and swaying in the wind of the open door, game, with legs knocked down.

He came out of his shop carefully, stepping into the street on the tips of his toes, as though someone might see or hear him. He crossed, and butting his forehead against the butcher's plate-glass front, stared at all the hooded eyes of the squabs, the withered collapsed webs of the ducks' feet, the choked scrap barrel, spilling out its lungs and guts. His stomach gave way, he was sick. He put his hand on the pit of his belly and pressed. He pulled at his beard, rolling the russet hairs that came away between his fingers.

He knew the butcher well; he also knew when he stepped out for a short beer at the saloon. He knew his habit of keeping the back door on the latch, he knew exactly what was stored in the back room. He expected no hindrance and got none. He pushed the back door in easily enough. For a moment the dimness left him blind, the next instant he emerged carrying a box. Now furtive, hurried, stumbling, he crossed back to his own door, opened it with his foot, and all but fell in.

The reflection of the ruby glass of the butcher's lamps ran red over his fashion-plates and strutting cardboard gentlemen. The little tailor put the box down in the farthest corner. His heart was beating high up in his neck. He groped about in his mind for something to stop at, some place to steady himself. He must make himself resolute. He clenched his chattering teeth, but it only made him cry. To stop that, he clasped both hands behind his neck, bending his neck down, and at the same time he sank to his knees beside the box and lowered his hands and forehead to the floor. He must do it! He must do it! He must do it *now*! His mind began its wandering again. He thought himself into his own country, in another season. Sunlight on the forest floor. He remembered the mosquitoes. He leaned back upon his heels, his arms hanging. The bright and sudden summer! Ploughing, seeding, the harvesting—what a pity it was. He paused, what was a pity? He only noticed it now!

Something moved in the box, breathing and kicking away from him; he uttered a cry, more grunt than cry, and the something in the box struck back with hard drumming fright.

The tailor bent forward, hands out, then he shoved them in between the slats of the box opening, shutting them tight! tight! tighter! The terrible, the really terrible thing, the creature does not squeal, wail, cry: it puffs, as if the wind were blunt; it thrashes its life, the frightful scuffling of the overwhelmed, in the last trifling enormity.

The tailor got to his feet, backing away from what he had done; he backed into the water pail, and turning, plunged his hands in. He beat the water, casting the waves up into his face with the heels of his hands. Then he went straight for the door and opened it. Addie fell face in, she had been standing straight up against the panel, her hands behind her back.

She righted herself without excuse or apology; she could tell by his face that he had done something enormous for the first time in his life, and without any doubt, for her. She came close to him, as she had to the door, her arms behind her. "What have you done?" she said.

"I—I have killed—I think I have killed—"

"Where? What?" She moved away from him, looking into the corner at the box. "*That!*" She began to laugh, harsh, back-bending laughter.

"Take it or leave it!" he shouted, and she stopped, her mouth open. She stooped and lifted up a small grey rabbit. She placed it on the table; then she came to Amietiev and wound her arms around him. "Come," she said. "Comb your hair."

She was afraid of him, there was something strange about his mouth swinging slightly sidewise. She was afraid of his walk, loud and flat. She pushed him toward the door. He placed one foot after the other, with a precision that brought the heel down first, the toe following . . .

"Where are you going?"

He did not seem to know where he was, he had forgotten her. He was shaking, his head straight up, his heart wringing wet.

She said tartly, "At least shine your boots!"

THE DOCTORS

"We have fashioned ourselves against the Day of Judgement." This remark was made by Dr. Katrina Silverstaff at the oddest moments, seeming without relevance to anything at all, as one might sigh, "Be still." Often she said it to herself. She thought it when on her way home, walking along the east wall of the river, dangling from her finger the loop of string about the box of seed cakes she always brought home for tea; but she always stopped to lean over the wall to watch the river barges, heavy with bright brick, moving off to the Islands.

Dr. Katrina, and her husband Dr. Otto, had been students in the same *gymnasium* at Freiburg-in-Breisgau. Both had started out for a doctorate in gynecology. Otto Silverstaff made it, as they say, but Katrina lost her way somewhere in vivisection, behaving as though she were aware of an impudence. Otto waited to see what she would do. She dropped out of class and was seen sitting in the park, bent forward, holding Otto's cane before her, its golden knob in both hands, her elbows braced on her legs, slowly poking the fallen leaves. She never recovered her gaiety. She married Otto but did not seem to know *when*; she knew why—she loved him—but he evaded her, by being in the stream of time; by being absolutely *daily*.

They came to America in the early twenties and were instantly enjoyed by the citizens of Second Avenue. The people liked them, they were trustworthy, they were durable; Doctor Katrina was useful to animal and birds, and Doctor Otto was, in his whole dedicated round little body, a man of fervor, who moved about any emergency with no dangling parts, aside from the rubber reins of his stethoscope. When he rapped his knuckles on a proffered back, he came around the shoulder with bulging eyes and puffing tense mouth, pronouncing verdict in heavy gusts of hope, licorice and carbolic acid.

The doctors' name plates stood side by side in the small tiled entry, and side by side (like people in a Dutch painting) the doctors sat at their table facing the window. The first day was the day she first remarked: "We have fashioned ourselves against the Day of Judgement." A globe of the world was between them, and at his side, a weighing machine. He had been idly pushing the balancing arm on its rusting teeth when she began speaking, and when she finished abruptly, he stopped, regarding her with a mild expression. He was inordinately pleased with her; she was "sea water" and "impersonal fortitude," neither asking for, nor needing attention. She was compact of dedicated merit, engaged in a mapped territory of abstraction, an excellently arranged encounter with estrangement; in short, she was to Otto incomprehensible, like a decision in chess, she could move to anything but whatever move, it appeared to the doctor, would be by the rules of that ancient game.

The doctors had been in office no more than a year when their first child was born, a girl, and in the year following, a boy; then no more children.

Now as Doctor Otto had always considered himself a liberal in the earlier saner sense of the word (as he would explain later, sitting with his neighbors in the Hungarian grill, his wife beside him), he found nothing strange in his wife's abstraction, her withdrawal, her silence, particularly if there was a xylophone and a girl, dancing on her boot's pivot, in the pungent air of the turning spit. Katrina had always been careful of music, note for note she can be said to have "attended." She collected books on comparative religions, too, and began learning Hebrew. He said to everybody, "So? are we not citizens of *anything*?"

Thus their life went into its tenth year. The girl had taken up dancing lessons, and the boy (wearing spectacles) was engrossed in insects. Then something happened that was quite extraordinary.

One day Doctor Katrina had opened the door to the ring of a travelling pedlar of books. As a rule, she had no patience with such fellows, and with a sharp "No, thank you!" would dismiss them. But this time she paused, the doorknob in her hand, and looked at a man who gave his name as Rodkin. He said that he was going all through that part of the city. He said that he had just missed it last year when he was selling Carlyle's *French Revolution*; this time however he was selling the Bible. Standing aside, Doctor Katrina let him pass. Evidently surprised, he did pass and stood in the hall.

"We will go into the waiting room," she said. "My husband is in consultation and must not be disturbed."

He said, "Yes, of course, I see." Though he did not see anything.

The waiting room was empty, dark and damp, like an acre risen from the sea. Doctor Katrina reached up and turned on a solitary light, which poured down its swinging arc upon the faded carpet.

The pedlar, a slight pale man with an uncurling flaxen beard, more like the beard of an animal than of a man, and with a shock of the same, almost white hair, hanging straight down from his crown, was—light eyes and all—hardly menacing; he was so colorless as to seem ghostly.

Doctor Katrina said, "We must talk about religion."

He was startled and asked why.

"Because," she said, "no one remembers it."

He did not answer until she told him to sit down, and he sat down, crossing his knees; then he said, "So?"

She sat opposite, her head slightly turned, apparently deliberating. Then she said, "I must have religion become out of the reach of the *few*, I mean out of reach *for* a few; something impossible again; to find again."

"*Become?*" he repeated, "that's a queer word."

"It is the only possible word," she said with irritation, "because, at the moment, religion is claimed by too many."

He ran a small hand through his beard. "Well, yes," he answered, "I see."

"No, you don't!" she rapped out sharply. "Let us come to the point. For me everything is too arranged. I'm not saying this because I need your help. I shall never need your help." She stared straight at him. "Understand that from the beginning."

"Beginning," he repeated in a loud voice.

"From the beginning, right from the start. Not help, *hindrance*."

"Accomplish what, Madame?" He took his hand away from his beard and lowered his left arm, dropping his books.

"That is my affair," she said, "it has nothing to do with you, you are only the means."

"So, so," he said. "The means."

A tremor ran off into her cheek, like a grimace of pain. "You can do nothing, not as a person." She stood up. "I must do it all. No!" she said, raising both hands, catching the ends of her shoulder scarf in a gesture of anger and pride, though he had not moved, "I shall be your mistress." She let her hands fall into the scarf's folds. "But," she added, "do not intrude. Tomorrow you will come to see me, that is enough; that is all." And with this "all," the little pedlar felt fear quite foreign to him.

However he came the next day, fumbling, bowing, stumbling. She would not see him. She sent word by the maid that she did not need him, and he went away abashed. He came again the day following, only to be told that Doctor Katrina Silverstaff was not in. The following Sunday she was.

She was quiet, almost gentle, as if she were preparing him for a disappointment, and he listened. "I have deliberately removed remorse from the forbidden; I hope you understand."

He said "Yes" and understood nothing.

She continued inexorably: "There will be no thorns for you. You will miss the thorns but do not presume to show it in my presence." Seeing his terror, she added: "And I do not permit you to suffer while I am in the room." Slowly and precisely, she began unfastening her brooch. "I dislike all spiritual decay."

"Oh, oh!" he said under his breath.

"It is the will," she said, "that must attain complete estrangement."

Without expecting to, he barked out, "I expect so."

She was silent, thinking, and he could not help himself, he heard his voice saying, "I want to suffer!"

She whirled around. "Not in my house."

"I will follow you through the world."

"I shall not miss you."

He said, "What will you do?"

"Does one destroy oneself when one is utterly disinterested?"

"I don't know."

Presently she said: "I love my husband. I want you to know that. It has nothing to do with this, still I want you to know it. I am *pleased* with him, and very proud."

"Yes, yes," Rodkin said, and began shaking again; his hand on the bedpost set the brasses ringing.

"There is something in me that is mournful because it is being."

He did not answer; he was crying.

"There's another thing," she said with harshness, "that I insist on—that you will not insult me by your attention while you are in the room."

He tried to stop his tears, and he tried to comprehend what was happening.

"You see," she continued, "some people drink poison, some take the knife, others drown. I take you."

In the dawn, sitting up, she asked him if he would smoke, and lit him a cigarette. After that she withdrew into herself, sitting on the edge of the mahogany board, her hands in her lap.

Unfortunately, there was new ease in Rodkin. He turned in bed, drawing his feet under his haunches, crossed, smoking slowly, carefully.

"Does one regret?"

Doctor Katrina did not answer, she did not move, she did not seem to have heard him.

"You frightened me last night," he said, pushing his heels out and lying on his back. "Last night I almost became somebody."

There was silence.

He began quoting from his Bible: "Shall the beasts of the field, the birds of the air forsake thee?" He added, "Shall any man forsake thee?"

Katrina Silverstaff remained as she was, but something under her cheek quivered.

The dawn broke, the streetlamps went out, a milk-cart rattled across the cobbles and into the dark of a side street.

"One. One out of many . . . *the* one."

Still, she said nothing, and he put his cigarette out. He was beginning to shiver; he rolled over and up, drawing on his clothes.

"When shall I see you again?" A cold sweat broke out over him, his hands shook. "Tomorrow?" He tried to come toward her, but he found himself at the door. "I'm nothing, nobody—" he turned toward her, bent slightly, as though he wished to kiss her, but no move helped him. "You are taking everything away. I can't feel—I don't suffer, nothing you know—I can't—" He tried to look at her. After a long time he succeeded.

He saw that she did not know he was in the room.

Then something like terror entered him, and with soft and cunning grasp, he turned the handle of the door and was gone.

A few days later, at dusk, his heart the heart of a dog, he came into the street of the doctors and looked at the house.

A single length of crêpe, bowed, hung at the door.

From that day he began to drink heavily. He became quite a nuisance in the cafés of the quarter; and once, when he saw Doctor Otto Silverstaff sitting alone in a corner with his two children, he laughed a loud laugh and burst into tears.

SMOKE

There was Swart with his bushy head and Fenken with the half-shut eyes and the grayish beard, and there also was Zelka with her big earrings and her closely bound inky hair, who had often been told that "she was very beautiful in a black way."

Ah, what a fine strong creature she had been, and what a fine strong creature her father, Fenken, had been before her, and what a specimen was her husband, Swart, with his gentle melancholy mouth and his strange strong eyes and his brown neck.

Fenken in his youth had loaded the cattle boats, and in his twilight of age he would sit in the round-backed chair by the open fireplace, his two trembling hands folded, and would talk of what he had been.

"A bony man I was, Zelka—my two knees as hard as a pavement, so that I clapped them with great discomfort to my own hands. Sometimes," he would add, with a twinkle in his old eyes, "I'd put you between them and my hand. It hurt less."

Zelka would turn her eyes on him slowly—they moved around into sight from under her eyebrows like the barrel of a well-kept gun; they were hard like metal and strong, and she was always conscious of them, even in sleep. When she would close her eyes before saying her prayers, she would remark to Swart, "I draw the hood over the artillery." And Swart would smile, nodding his large head.

In the town these three were called the "Bullets"— when they came down the street, little children sprang aside, not because they were afraid, but because they came so fast and brought with them something so healthy, something so potent, something unconquerable. Fenken could make his fingers snap against his palm like the crack of a cabby's whip just by shutting his hand abruptly, and he did this often, watching the gamin and smiling.

Swart, too, had his power, but there was a hint at something softer in him, something that made the lips kind when they were sternest, something that gave him a sad expression when he was thinking—something that had drawn Zelka to him in their first days of courting. "We Fenkens," she would say, "have iron in our veins—in yours I fear there's a little blood."

Zelka was cleanly. She washed her linen clean as though she were punishing the dirt. Had the linen been less durable there would have been holes in it from her knuckles in six months. Everything Zelka cooked was tender—she had bruised it with her preparations.

And then Zelka's baby had come. A healthy, fat, little crying thing, with eyes like its father's and with its father's mouth. In vain did Zelka look for something about it that would give it away as one of the Fenken blood—it had a maddeningly tender way of stroking her face; its hair was finer than blown gold; and it squinted up its pale blue eyes when it fell over its nose. Sometimes Zelka would turn the baby around in bed, placing its little feet against her side, waiting for it to kick. And when it finally did, it was gently and without great strength and with much good humor. "Swart," Zelka would say, "your child is entirely human. I'm afraid all his veins run blood." And she would add to her father, "Sonny will never load the cattle ships."

When it was old enough to crawl, Zelka would get down on hands and knees and chase it about the little ash-littered room. The baby would crawl ahead of her, giggling and driving Zelka mad with a desire to stop and hug him. But when she roared behind him like a lion to make him hurry, the baby would roll over slowly, struggle into a sitting posture, and, putting his hand up, would sit staring at her as though he would like to study out something that made this difference between them.

When it was seven, it would escape from the house and wander down to the shore, and stand for hours watching the boats coming in, being loaded and unloaded. Once one of the men put the cattle belt about him and lowered him into the boat. He went down sadly, his little golden head drooping and his feet hanging down. When they brought him back on shore again and dusted him off, they were puzzled at him—he had neither cried nor laughed. They said, "Didn't you like that?" And he had only answered by looking at them fixedly.

And when he grew up, he was very tender to his mother, who had taken to shaking her head over him. Fenken had died the summer of his grandchild's thirtieth year, so that after the funeral Swart had taken the round-backed chair for his own. And now he sat there with folded hands, but he never said what a strong lad he had been. Sometimes he would say, "Do you remember how Fenken used to snap his fingers together like a whip?" And Zelka would answer, "I do."

And finally, when her son married, Zelka was seen at the feast dressed in a short blue skirt, leaning upon Swart's arm, both of them still strong and handsome and capable of lifting the buckets of cider.

Zelka's son had chosen a strange woman for a wife: a little thin thing, with a tiny waistline and a narrow chest and a small, very lovely throat. She was the daughter of a ship owner and had a good deal of money in her name. When she married Zelka's son, she brought him some ten thousand a year. And so he stopped the shipping of cattle and went in for exports and imports of Oriental silks and perfumes.

When his mother and father died, he moved a little inland away from the sea and hired clerks to do his bidding. Still, he never forgot what his mother had said to him: "There must always be a little iron in the blood, sonny."

He reflected on this when he looked at Lief, his wife. He was a silent, taciturn man as he grew older, and Lief had grown afraid of him, because of his very kindness and his melancholy.

There was only one person to whom he was a bit stern, and this was his daughter, "Little Lief." Toward her he showed a strange hostility, a touch even of that fierceness that had been his mother's. Once she had rushed shrieking from his room because he had suddenly roared behind her as his mother had done behind him. When she was gone, he sat for a long time by his table, his hands stretched out in front of him, thinking.

He had succeeded well. He had multiplied his wife's money now into the many thousands—they had a house in the country and servants. They were spoken of in the town as a couple who had an existence that might be termed as "pretty soft"; and when the carriage drove by of a Sunday with baby Lief up front on her mother's lap and Lief's husband beside her in his gray cloth coat, they stood aside not to be trampled on by the swift legged, slender ankled "pacer" that Lief had bought that day when she had visited the "old home"—the beach that had known her and her husband when they were children. This horse was the very one that she had asked for when she saw how beautiful it was as they fastened the belt to it preparatory to lowering it over the side. It was then that she remembered how, when her husband had been a little boy, they had lowered him over into the boat with this same belting.

During the winter that followed, which was a very hard one, Lief took cold and resorted to hot water bottles and thin tea. She became very fretful and annoyed at her husband's constant questionings as to her health. Even Little Lief was a nuisance because she was so noisy. She would steal into the room, and, crawling under her mother's bed, would begin to sing in a high, thin treble, pushing the ticking with her patent leather boots to see them crinkle. Then the mother would cry out, the nurse would run in and take her away, and Lief would spend a half hour in tears. Finally, they would not allow Little Lief in the room, so she would steal by the door many times, walking noiselessly up and down the hall. But finally, her youth overcoming her, she would stretch her legs out into a straight goose step, and for this she was whipped because on the day that she had been caught, her mother had died.

And so, the time passed, and the years rolled on, taking their toll. It was now many summers since that day that Zelka had walked into town with Swart—now many years since Fenken had snapped his fingers like a cabby's whip. Little Lief had never even heard that her grandmother had been called a "beautiful woman in a black sort of way," and she had only vaguely heard of the nickname that had once been given the family, the "Bullets." She came to know that great strength had once been in the family to such an extent, indeed, that somehow a phrase was known to her, "Remember always to keep a little iron in the blood." And one night she had pricked her arm to see if there were iron in it, and she had cried because it hurt. And so, she knew that there was none.

With her this phrase ended. She never repeated it because of that night when she had made that discovery.

Her father had taken to solitude and the study of sociology. Sometimes he would turn her about by the shoulder and look at her, breathing in a thick way he had with him of late. And once he told her she was a good girl but foolish, he left her alone.

They had begun to lose money, and some of Little Lief's tapestries, given her by her mother, were sold. Her heart broke, but she opened the windows oftener because she needed some kind of beauty. She made the mistake of loving tapestries best and nature second best. Somehow, she had gotten the two things mixed—of course, it was due to her bringing up. "If you are poor, you live out-of-doors; but if you are rich, you live in a lovely house." So to her the greatest of calamities had befallen the house. It was beginning to go away by those imperceptible means that at first leave a house looking unfamiliar and then bare.

Finally, she could stand it no longer and she married a thin, wiry man with a long, thin nose and a nasty trick of rubbing it with a finger equally long and thin—a man with a fair income and very refined sisters.

This man, Misha, wanted to be a lawyer. He studied half the night and never seemed happy unless his head was in his palm. His sisters were like this also, only for another reason: they enjoyed weeping. If they could find nothing to cry about, they cried for the annoyance of this dearth of destitution and worry. They held daily councils for future domestic trouble—one the gesture of emotional and one of mental desire.

Sometimes Little Lief's father would come to the big iron gate and ask to see her. He would never come in— why? He never explained. So Little Lief and he would talk over the gate top, and sometimes he was gentle and sometimes he was not. When he was harsh to her, Little Lief wept, and when she wept, he would look at her steadily from under his eyebrows and say nothing. Sometimes, he asked her to take a walk with him. This would set Little Lief into a terrible flutter; the corners of her mouth would twitch and her nostrils tremble. But she always went.

Misha worried little about his wife. He was a very selfish man, with that greatest capacity of a selfish nature, the ability to labor untiringly for some one thing that he wanted, and that nature had placed beyond his reach. Some people called this quality excellent, pointing out what a great scholar Misha was, holding him up as an example in their own households, looking after him when he went hurriedly down the street with that show of nervous expectancy that a man always betrays when he knows within himself that he is deficient—a sort of peering in the face of life to see if it has discovered the flaw.

Little Lief felt that her father was trying to be something that was not natural to him. What was it? As she grew older, she tried to puzzle it out. Now it happened more often that she would catch him looking at her in a strange way, and once she asked him half playfully if he wished she had been a boy. And he had answered abruptly, "Yes, I do."

Little Lief would stand for hours at the casement and, leaning her head against the glass, try to solve this thing about her father. And then she discovered it when he had said, "Yes, I do." He was trying to be strong—what was it that was in the family?—oh, yes—iron in the blood. He feared there was no longer any iron left. Well, perhaps there wasn't—was that the reason he looked at her like this? No, he was worried about himself. Why?—wasn't he satisfied with his own strength? He had been cruel enough very often. This shouldn't have worried him.

She asked him, and he answered, "Yes, but cruelty isn't strength." That was an admission. She was less afraid of him since that day when he had made that answer, but now she kept peering into his face as he had done into hers, and he seemed not to notice it. Well, he was getting to be a very old man.

Then one day her two sisters-in-law pounced upon her so that her golden head shook on its thin, delicate neck.

"Your father has come into the garden," cried one.

"Yes, yes," pursued the elder. "He's even sat himself upon the bench."

She hurried out to him. "What's the matter, father?" Her head was aching.

"Nothing." He did not look up.

She sat down beside him, stroking his hand, at first timidly, then with more courage.

"Have you looked at the garden?"

He nodded.

She burst into tears.

He took his hand away from her and began to laugh.

"What's the matter, child? A good dose of hog-killing would do you good."

"You have no right to speak to me in this way—take yourself off!" she cried sharply, holding her side. And her father rocked with laughter.

She stretched her long, thin arms out, clenching her thin fingers together. The lace on her short sleeves trembled, her knuckles grew white.

"A good pig-killing," he repeated, watching her. And she grew sullen.

"Eh?" He pinched her flesh a little and dropped it. She was passive; she made no murmur. He got up, walked to the gate, opened it and went out, closing it after him. He turned back a step and waved to her. She did not answer for a moment, then she waved back slowly with one of her thin, white hands.

She would have liked to refuse to see him again, but she lacked courage. She would say to herself, "If I am unkind to him now, perhaps later I shall regret it." In this way she tried to excuse herself. The very next time he had sent word that he wished speech with her, she had come.

"Little fool!" he said, in a terrible rage, and walked off. She was quite sure that he was slowly losing his mind—a second childhood, she called it, still trying to make things as pleasant as possible.

She had been ill a good deal that spring, and in the fall, she had terrible headaches. In the winter months she took to her bed, and early in May the doctor was summoned.

Misha talked to the physician in the drawing-room before he sent him up to his wife.

"You must be gentle with her. She is nervous and frail." The doctor laughed outright. Misha's sisters were weeping, of course, and perfectly happy.

"It will be such a splendid thing for her," they said, meaning the beef, iron and wine that they expected the doctor to prescribe.

Toward evening Little Lief closed her eyes.

Her child was still-born.

The physician came downstairs and entered the parlor where Misha's sisters stood together, still shedding tears.

He rubbed his hands.

"Send Misha upstairs."

"He has gone."

"Isn't it dreadful? I never could bear corpses, especially little ones."

"A baby isn't a corpse," answered the physician, smiling at his own impending humor. "It's an interrupted plan."

He felt that the baby, not having drawn a breath in this world, could not feel hurt at such a remark, because it had gathered no feminine pride and, also, as it had passed out quicker than the time it took to make the observation, it really could be called nothing more than the background for medical jocularity.

Misha came into the room with red eyes.

"Out like a puff of smoke," he said.

One of the sisters remarked: "Well, the Fenkens lived themselves thin."

The next summer Misha married into a healthy Swedish family. His second wife had a broad face, with eyes set wide apart, and with broad, flat, healthy, yellow teeth. And she played the piano surprisingly well, though she looked a little heavy as she sat upon the piano stool.

THE TERRORISTS

In early youth Pilaat had been very melancholy, though vigorous. This was due to his healthy body and to his imaginative mind.

Those people who are in the habit of assuming that a melancholy stomach must accompany a sad mind, were rather disconcerted with Pilaat's indomitable digestion, about his excesses that never gave him punishment in their passing, and about his unalterable decision to become a necessity in the community.

Then his hair had been long and his dress decidedly on the "artistic" plan. His straight nose had below it a very full and perhaps weak mouth, and above it, eyes of a strange, large and mournful turn.

Time shortened the hair a little and the mouth was covered by a graying mustache. The eyes watered easily, and sometimes, during an evening, blood veins would stretch across them.

Pilaat was no longer vigorous, though for a man of fifty odd, he was robust enough. On the other hand, his melancholy had, so people seemed to think, disappeared altogether. Those who knew him longest made the mistake of calling him "more like a human being"; and those who knew him the shortest made the correct judgment, that he was "drinking too much."

His early love of the people had sent him toward them eagerly. Being close to them and in with them, he learned how pitifully weak they all were, and his strong digestion made him despise them for those qualities that, somehow, he blamed on environment and not heredity, excepting as one can inherit the filth of the gutter and the starvation of the ash pile. And along with his interest, his study and his acknowledgment of its inevitability, came this robust hate.

From speaking of the people as the "Unfortunate," he spoke of them as the "Miserable." And in the way he said this word there was no sound of pity for their sad, shabby hearts; there was only a knowledge that their garments were also shabby and mournful. Had Pilaat come from a less cleanly family, he would have loved them very strongly and gently to the end. But he had been comforted and maimed in his conceptions and his fellow love by too many clean shirts in youth. He still longed to correct things, but he wanted to correct them as one cleans up a floor, not as one binds up a wound.

He shouted because his heart was heavy. He began to awe those of his own group. Soon enough, they called him the "Terrorist," and, in the end, when he made a gesture of pity, people raised their arms to protect themselves.

He had a very young wife, a weak-chinned, small thing about 27 years old. She had been nicknamed Joan d'Arc, because of a certain pale loveliness about the frail oblong of her face. She had lost two or three teeth, and she smoked innumerable cigarettes, drank beer on half-holidays, and flirted with anyone whom she despised.

She believed in the vanity of all things and the pessimism in all things, and she wanted to annihilate any slovenly ease of mind in herself, so she deliberately set about annihilating her own soul and her own delicate, sensitive, and keen insight.

She wore heavy boots that seemed to be drawing her down; thus her five feet looked like three.

Her hair was cut short after the manner of intellectuals among the women of her set, and she wore loose and dirty blouses, smeared with paint and oil.

She was in the cafés all the afternoon from three till six, when she "cleared out" for "the pigs," the smug and respectable who brought their wives and children to dine. Again, at nine she was back talking about the revolutionists.

Pilaat had written some poems and had them published obscurely; these she always carried around with her, reading them aloud or studying them nonchalantly. She had long grown tired of them, but she wanted to puzzle the strangers who filtered in, and she wanted to add, when asked about them, "By Pilaat Korb—you know, the Terrorist," never referring to the fact that he was her husband; this she left for others to whisper. She liked to be the center of whispers, for then she could be impersonal and forget herself without any danger of falling into obscurity.

Among her friends she would permit herself the pleasure of pretending to feel human suffering very deeply. She would swing her arms about, imitating Pilaat. She would lean far back in her chair as he did when he had finished a sentence, as "I know, you call me crazy—but that is not all. I have a retort to make, an accusation. You, the people—what do you know?—are you not being swindled on every side, and yet you submit? Ah, fools! Fools!" he would shout. "You are always horribly conscious of your bones, and you begin to think that it is as it should be. You say this is life—bah!" He would then end up leaning far back as his wife did when she copied him, thinking that she was expressing herself. And sometimes her friends said, "Certainly, there you are," while they drank beer or devoured large, ill-shaped sandwiches.

She would say, "You wander, my poor friends, about the world like shadows. We must find you your bodies once again." She said "we" with that intonation used by agitators.

These two lived in a dismal little garret high above the rest of the sad houses of the shabby side street. The building had once been some kind of church or house of devotion, but had long ago been turned into rooms, and was now frequented by a vocalist, a violin and piano teacher, and a few out-at-knee artists.

There was never any lock on the outer door, approached by three rickety steps. Two or three iron mailboxes clung to the walls, and in the winter, when the wind howled hardest and the snow made park benches impossible, tramps and derelicts of all kinds would creep in here and sleep along the walls near the dry wood of the steps.

Their garret had been at one time very dignified and almost elegant, as its tall lines and its heavy wood proclaimed. Its windows and the architecture of the roof spoke of a past that had been no mean thing. Now it was like a woman who had fallen from wealth and distinction and esteem, who had lost all her admirers, but not quite all her looks, who passes her remaining days in that odd mixture of clothes that look so strange together—a silk and beribboned petticoat hidden by a calico dressing gown, a torn stocking thrust into small and delightfully fashioned slippers, a well-appointed mouth closing on crumbs. Such was the room to which of an evening Pilaat and his little wife climbed.

Sometimes the sleeping men in the hall would be awakened by their late arrival and would turn over muttering abuse, or some of them accepted Pilaat's invitation to have a drink with him.

Thus he would collect a party that often made merry until the small hours of the morning. Or Pilaat would bring some of his friends with him—they led the life of actors—sleeping into the late afternoon and staying up half or all of the night.

Toward the end of his career, Pilaat began to tear his mustache out. When remonstrated with, he would say, "I am preparing to show my teeth." He had become very nervous and excitable and unhappy. He felt that the world was not going in the direction that he had wished. It neither turned toward his solution early enough, nor did it, on the other hand, succumb to its final end, as he had predicted, soon enough for him. He was tired of living out his life and watching others live out theirs on the prescribed gradual plan. He was annoyed with the passage of time; it infuriated him that twenty-four hours were still a day and that there were seven days a week, as there had been when he was born.

He no longer wrote poetry or plays, nor did he keep up his connection with a paper which he had started, and which spoke harshly of all things. He had taken more and more to his bottle, and because he was very nervous, he drank too much, and because he drank too much, he became more and more excitable.

Instead of writing his poetry, now he laid it in among the strands of his wife's hair in his occasional tender strok-ing, when he would call her Little One and, sometimes, Sniffle Snuffle, when he would burst out laughing heartily at her disconcerted countenance. She knew well enough that Pilaat saw through her would-be ferocity and her assumed interest in the world. After all, she was only a little girl who, because she was interested, thought that she must assume fury, and because she was too lazy to dress her hair after the fashion, cut it off.

Yet there was something strange about Pilaat's wife. She did not like the society of silly and vain women, and she did turn most naturally to such men as her husband moved among. Perhaps it started in a torn shoe and a con-sciousness that only in such society are shoes valued more for the pass they have come to than for what they had been originally.

•

She had never much sympathy for "society," and a marriage of money disgusted her, though her family had, in the beginning, some such vain ideas about her. They were respectable people who owned a little estate somewhere near the sea, and who had been dropped in successive generations into the midst of old and tarnished jewelry comprising the family splendor. Most of this they had given to their daughter when they had their first ambitions in the way of a well-to-do doctor in the village, and which their daughter had promptly pawned. Sometimes, it is true, this jewelry would come back, piece by piece, and appear on her wrist or about her neck or from her ears, and at such times she drew a little aside from her husband and his friends, and would sit dreaming in a corner, her red wrists about her little crooked knees.

On one such night as this Pilaat had acted very strangely indeed. He had passed several morose hours by himself, and finally at a café located his wife, wearing this mysterious and migratory jewelry.

The sight of these gems and silvers always put him into a passion either of avarice or contempt—he would get hold of them and realize money on the spot, or he would very bitterly place them on the table before him and solemnly demand that they be cleared away with the rest of the "rubbish."

His wife would become silent, smiling a little, her head thrown back. Or, if the waiter did make a motion to sweep the trinkets away, she would say in a loud voice, "Yes, that's right: take them away. Feed them to the chickens or make a meal off them. I'm tired of supporting them." Then Pilaat cried in a terrible fury, catching the dazed waiter by the wrist and swearing at the top of his voice in Rumanian, Italian and French, saying that he was being treated like a man "who has not come honestly by his decorations."

From this, he went off into a melancholy reverie. He answered nothing in the way of a question and ordered innumerable bottles of wine.

When, accompanied by three or four friends, they finally reached their house, Pilaat threatened to kill the vocalist who was teaching someone to sing in the room below them, it being half-past twelve.

"What is all that racket about?" he demanded, flying down the steps and pounding on the door of the vocalist's room. A thin, yellow-faced woman, the vocalist in question, opened the door sharply, thrust her head out, and said: "Be off with you, you lazy vagabond. In my country such people as you would be locked up."

Pilaat struck his chest with his fist. "Locked up, is it?" he demanded, smiling fiercely. "Locked up, is it? That is what I have against this country. They do not let you go home unless you commit something that makes you a little ashamed to say, 'How do you do?' to the mother of all things, the cell."

She slammed the door on the implication. "You're crazy!" Pilaat flew back upstairs, shouting: "Crazy! and did I not warn you that I was crazy, you poor, senseless thing? Did I not give myself full credit for it in the very beginning? But does that make it necessary for me to be tortured with the horrible sounds issuing from such lovely throats as Maria's [the pupil who took the vocal lessons]? And must I forever regret the inferiority of the things Maria is forced to swallow, and of the noise Maria tosses from out her little throat?"

He was in the middle of the room by this time, and much amused his friends. His wife leaned back in the corner and twisted the bracelets around and around, blinking her eyelids and shuffling with her feet.

"What is it you would do with the little Maria if you had her and could dispose of her case as you would, eh?" inquired one man, with a bristling beard and an odor about him of tar.

"What would I do?" demanded Pilaat, seating himself with his back to the fire. "I would have her singing in Paradise by dawn. After all, I am a man of force. Someday I shall march upon the town and shall show you. It's about time for an uprising when little girls think they can sing, and young men think they can govern."

"Ah, well, it's a dull season; the autumn is nearly here."

"Autumn," retorted Pilaat, flourishing his arm, "is the season for destruction—but we are weak, miserable creatures, and we leave to nature all the tearing down of the scenery, and to her we leave all the building up of the same scenery next year and the year after for interminable and tireless and wearisome years."

"Well?"

"I would tear down the scenery better than all of them," he said irrelevantly. "Than all of them I would rip the whole existing plan of nature to pieces. How she would shiver, how she would implore. But I should have no mercy. No, not even when she got upon her knees and wept at my feet and covered them with her insufferable tears. I would invite her to suicide. I would mock at the stains upon her cheeks. I would glory at the dirt on the imploring knees. I would laugh aloud, and shake her by those horrible, ample shoulders of hers, and would cry out to her, 'Now die, die; we do not care! Tear the little leaves out of your heart. We are in need of them for a bed. Weep; we need a drink. Destroy yourself, for we need a harp on which to sing the song of freedom.'" He had become half drunk with his frenzy, and he stood up.

"I tell you, I would say to her: 'We are tired of you. I, Pilaat, am tired of you, and she, my little girl, is tired of you, and Maria is tired of you. We are tired of your spontaneity and your persistency and your punctuality. We want to see you dead and smoldering. What will we do? We will thrust our feet into your heart because they are cold, and our hands we will warm at your palms. And we will shake them at your death, saying: "At last you have accomplished more than seasons and beauty; you have created destruction." We can no longer rise in the morning and say, "Behold, the sun has arisen." We shall no longer send our children to school to learn mathematics. We shall never be connected with you any longer as the outcome of your whims. We are set free—thus.'" He snapped his fingers and executed a pirouette on his heel, and sat down, discussing the feasibility of destruction on a large scale.

•

His wife still blinked her eyes in the corner, and continued to roll her bracelets. The whole room had such a menacing aspect, such a sad and gloomy atmosphere, and contained so many odors and voices that she was annoyed and wanted to sleep. Sleep had overcome one of the men who leaned against a table; his head had fallen forward and he snored a little.

In the other corner of the room, the conversation had taken a decidedly revolutionary turn. They were beginning to talk of besieging the town. Names were mentioned as persons to destroy. They began to collect things that would do as missiles.

The room began to bristle. Dark beards stood out as though their wearers had been scratched. Lips protruded, ears trembled, the very beards began to shake. Fists doubled up, eyes sparkled, and the tongue knew no forbidden thing. There was something at once terrible and beautiful about these men, who, rising, suddenly turned for a moment toward the old boards of that room such a searching and melancholy gaze that tatters and misery might have seemed for one instant something splendid.

"Eh, it will be magnificent. In the dawn we shall do it. In the dawn we shall creep forth to make the world better for men. They will see us coming, creeping on all fours, and they will say, 'Here are the rats.' They shall learn what rats can do." Some of the men stretched a little among the empty bottles. Pilaat began to drowse, a heavy paperweight in his hand. John, his bosom friend, leaned near with the broken leg of a chair firmly clutched in his hand, and he whispered a little to make it more menacing.

·

The fire had died down and barely a light flickered. Pilaat's head fell forward on his chest. The bristling beards one by one relaxed and rested once more down in smooth, silky lines. Deep breathing took the place of cries, oaths, imprecations. Pilaat's wife stirred uneasily in her corner, dreaming, her hand over her bracelets.

She woke up—it was midday. She looked out into the street. A postman was standing on the steps of the door opposite, and a woman with a baby in pink ribbons moved slowly out toward the park.

She stumbled over Pilaat and two or three of the men huddled together for warmth. All of them, in their sleep, had moved away from those things that they had collected as weapons. They had rolled onto them, and they found that they hurt and were uncomfortable. The chair leg lay beside the paperweight. She stretched, opened her mouth, and yawned. She looked about for a cigarette stub, and found it, lighting it slowly. She prepared the little oil stove for the reception of the old and stained coffeepot. She looked out of the window again; it was a splendid day. She thought of her favorite café, and she smiled as she contemplated one or two new phrases she would use in relation to life. She put Pilaat's book in her pocket. The coffee began to boil.

WHO IS THIS TOM SCARLETT?

He snarls.

It is a philosophy; one's lower teeth are always good.

On either side of him sit three men.

The room is long, narrow, and the heavy smoke creeps up and down, touching first one, then another, shuddering off. Seven bowls of soup stand at regular intervals upon the table. The imprint of foreign hostelries is upon the silver. On the walls, just behind the seven heads, are seven blue and white Dutch plates like halos, and above the seven plates the rising and placating star, a liquor license.

Tom Scarlett turns his face from side to side, brushing his shoulders as he does so with the ends of his long black sideburns. Like a bird whose wings have been plucked of their flight, this fall of hair seems to have been robbed of its support, clinging to the mouth, which is raised diagonally across fine yellow teeth. The head is magnificent and bald. Like a woman who is so beautiful that clothes instinctively fall from her, this head has risen above its hair in a moment of abandon known only to men who have drawn their feet out of their boots to walk awhile in the corridors of the mind.

His hands lie in front of him. They are long, white, convalescent hands, on which the dew of death is always apparent, the knuckles interrupting each pale space with a sudden symmetrical line of bone. These hands lie between the anchovies and the salt, and as he turns first to the right and then to the left, they move imperceptibly, as though reins were attached to them from the head. And as Tom Scarlett snarls, Tash laughs.

Spave torments a pickle that lies in front of him with a fork, squirting drops of green juice upon the bare boards. Some of the others talk of a person of bad repute. One calls loudly for a glass of rum, while the sixth breaks, one after another, the backs of toothpicks, littering them over the floor.

They have been jesting among themselves because Tom Scarlett has been lonely again. They tell him that he has too many interests, and he answers: "Should one pass you over with nose keen for the most fragrant portion of your souls, where the flowers of your persistency have left their perfume, that nose would stop between your first and second knuckle, for on your smoke you have concentrated, as I on my flame."

They look at one another, and move among themselves, and finally are swept away in a great gale of laughter, whereat Tom Scarlett snarls and lets his face fall back into its habitual calmness.

The clock in the street strikes three. In the tolling of the bell the six hear the voice of their trade. For Tom

Scarlett alone does it strike off another morning in man's short life.

For Spave it means that his counter is waiting his cheating barter; for Glaub, that the little pigs in his rotisserie lie feet upward in anticipation of the spit that shall be a staff on which to climb to the eminence of man's stomach; while for Shrive the ink is drying in his bottles used so illy to amuse men; and for Tash that the lumber in his yard is growing gray in the rain. Freece seems to see his oils drying upon his canvas; while, last of all, it recalls to Umbas' mind the fact that there are three pretty little corpses waiting to be sent to heaven with becoming smiles upon their lips and a yard or two of lace bought at a great reduction from a dealer on Second Avenue, because slightly damaged, when his wife called him a fool and his hand shook.

To hurry matters, the six crane their necks in the direction of the kitchen, where Lizette is making sauce for the spaghetti. They cannot see, however, because Madame is sitting at her table drinking wine and snarling at her dog, and from time to time reaching down to rub forefinger and thumb in its hair, as though its fleas were her torment also. Tom Scarlett has often wondered how she kept her diners, so morose she is and so bitter. Her eyebrows twitch over her eyes like long black whips goading her eyeballs on to hate and menace.

Spave balances an almond on his polished fingernail and sends it up, up, spinning into the air, where it turns, striking Madame's glass, dashing a blot of red upon the tablecloth. Madame opens her mouth, the eyebrows raise themselves as if to strike.

Spave leans forward, extending a stick of celery. "For your little teeth," he says, and Madame's jaws snap to like a grate.

But Tom Scarlett is annoyed, and because he is annoyed, he realizes that he is different. Madame's eyes have become gamin; they search the men, darting here and there. One would say that they concealed a tongue, hid a mouth, cloaked a fist. Madame is always one course ahead of her diners. She seems to derive a great deal of pleasure from the fact. She is especially pleased if she can have one dish that they will not get at all.

The dog, like his mistress, is bad tempered in a tricky way, standing with one paw upon a bone—one morsel ahead of the yellow cur sniffing by the lintel. Sometimes this dog smiles, the saliva running in a silver rim around his lips, dropping tear-wise slowly.

Tom Scarlett and the dog have something in common; both reproduce the atmosphere under which they serve— the one his mistress and the other his time.

Who is this, Tom Scarlett?

His friends have ceased to idolize him because they have caught him picking his teeth. Thus many deities take the toboggan. They no longer marvel at him because he has given them to eat of the fruit of his soul—and because it was tropical and strange and they could not eat it, they said it was not eatable. Tom Scarlett snarls and offers them cigars, which they are more than glad to get.

"You are like a steak," they tell him; "good only when digested."

Tash beats upon his vest and howls.

"How you will be appreciated when his stomach has appropriated you."

Tom Scarlett answers quietly: "Still, I shall be the dish."

"But we the approval. A great man should keep several stomachs as he keeps a wine chest."

Tears bulge out Tom Scarlett's eyelids, but he answers gently: "I stand alone among men."

"So the flower thinks."

"Well?"

"There are always dead flowers to nourish the living, as there are always dead minds to support the steps of greatness."

Tom Scarlett smiles, exposing his fine teeth.

"I have crawled around the rim of the world like a fly—I know what I know." He leaned forward, placing his finger on Tash. "If men," he said, ruminatively, "were forty feet taller, the screaming of those in death would sound like crickets chirruping in the grass in the evening. The greatest kiss would be but a little puckering, which, when interrupted, would give out a fleshy sigh." He tosses up his hands, laughing greatly down the hairs of his beard.

"You will die as others die."

He answers: "Yes, I shall die as others die—crying out. But here I shall differ. A great man gives birth to himself; for him the death rattle is the wail of birth."

Spave spits: "He will put his hand upon his stomach as one in mortal pain, but he will cry, 'My head! My head!' A last transaction in favor of the mind."

And so, they grew merry tormenting him.

One day they came later than usual. Madame was not drinking; instead, she kept passing her hand back and forth across her dog's spine. She scowled, it is true, giving the room more of its usual morose aspect, thereby maintaining its cheerful air—for only by maintaining established custom are we entirely content. Still, she shook her head in a way that seemed to give her a good deal of sorrow.

And they shook themselves because it was raining outside, a peculiar dampness that suggests to mind the fact that all things must attach themselves to some ailment, even men, reminded them that the earth draws much back to herself in her rainstorms besides the growing river and the autumn leaves. So they shuddered, and Madame, eating her Parmesan, shuddered also and spoke to them.

"He is walking again today."

She pointed upward, for Tom Scarlett lodged on the parlor floor.

"Ah, he will be down presently."

"I do not think so."

"You will see. One's stomach is always the gendarme of one's mind."

"But listen."

Five of them try to, but Race, taking his coat off, knocks over a chair.

"Why in the name of the saints can't you be quiet?" they shouted, in the exasperated manner of men who, if thwarted in their silences, will at least not be thwarted in their uproars.

"It's well," said Madame, peeling an apple; "You could not hear him, anyway; one has to see him now."

"What is wrong?"

"He walks like a cat. Do you remember what a noise he used to make with his great feet, as though he wanted the furniture to know he approached." She clicked her tongue. "No more."

The six began at their soup. "He will come down, you will see." But when he failed to come at the appearance of the cheese and nuts, they began to talk among themselves. They said, "What can this be?" And they said, "He has indeed altered: I no longer hear his great feet upon the boards. He had arrogant feet."

Old Tash chuckled.

"After all, in a monarchy or in a republic, it's us little men that count. We bear the children, then we sense that one among the lot is different. Is it not by our hand that its face is kept clean? Would it not be a dirty gamin running around the streets in tatters, holding up its hands to squint at the stars, but walking in prodigious puddles? Is it not our care that keeps the bib dry? Do we not hide our children's drool until they are old enough to hide it for themselves? And is it not by our hand that the child is fed, that he is brought up into manhood? Don't we print his books, don't we build his colleges, don't we sweep his streets, light his lamps, make his bed, and in the end is it not us who bury him, after building him that other house that he has peradventure to leave; and is it not we who write his biography? He may be the voice, but who are the ears? Eh? He may paint the pictures, but who are the eyes? He may be a rare flower, but who is the nose? He may have his head in the clouds, but who is the earth in which his feet are set?"

He gave vent to a loud, rich laugh, a laugh that wedged its way between much good eating to reach the ears of Madame. He leaned back, striking his vest, as a jockey strikes his horse, letting his breath escape him in that after-dinner sigh indulged in by the rotund. "After all is said and done, Madame, is it not we, I ask you, who are the great importance of the earth?"

Madame raised her eyebrows.

"He walks like a cat. I do not like it."

"So softly?"

"So softly, little dusty footfalls, like a cat, a small, profound cat. Men walk that way when they have changed their minds."

She did not explain what she meant by the word profound.

"A little, dusty cat, with a gray nose from prowling in among what people call great facts. Why, will you tell me, have all great things to be dusted? Cathedrals and books and windmills?"

They lit their cigars.

Madame snapped: "Eh, eh, and bric-a-brac and the inside of all empty bowls, the floors of reservoirs have known the feet of the sparrows."

"You talk in riddles, Madame."

"I talk one language; you hear another."

"The dog wants a bone," they suggested, and assumed a calm mien.

They asked Glaub about his rotisserie, and why he did not eat of his own little pigs for a change.

He answered: "Can one eat his own child? The aroma from my little pigs is like a sigh going up to heaven; it almost placates me. No, no," he added, "I cannot eat my little pigs; others must do that for me. We leave our children's seasoning to the public; they are the ones who make them tender and profitable. So with my little bits of pork with features at one end and a little exclamation point of a tail at the other. It is a waste of nature's talents that she gives features to her meats, but there it is."

"There are some who say that the odor of a butcher's shop is delicious—and fattening."

Glaub shuddered.

Like buzzards these six had flapped about the life of Tom Scarlett in that little basement room where Madame served her persistent table d'hôte, and as such carrion swoop down and take away the eyes of the dead that have been its light, they swooped down upon the brilliancies of Tom Scarlett, thinking, animal-like, that they had its radiance between their teeth. But it was only the empty husk of a thought because they could not understand.

For long months they had tormented him so. For many long months they had been content to eat food that was at best a hollow mockery, as such food is liable to be. But to Tom Scarlett there was some dire truth in what they said—for he realized that around and around such men as he circled such a six and such another six interminably; and Tom Scarlett knew that because of him they gathered undue radiance.

So today when Madame failed to drink her red wine, while she rubbed the back of her dog and scowled and would say nothing to them that was either hard and biting, or soft and unctuous, they were uncomfortable. Was it not raining outside, and had not dampness settled down to a tête-à-tête with the smoke that hung like a yellow rag before the nose of each as they picked their teeth?

Shrive took another sip of wine. "If this country," he was saying in a garrulous tone to Glaub at his left, "does not give more chance to its public men—eh, I admit," he added hastily at the opening of Glaub's mouth, "that there should be places for the men of importance, of course, like the President and the deans of colleges and strikebreakers, but there should be one or two exalted chairs for its minor poets and its journalists. We can't all have a great man on ice."

The other four heard the last part of the speech and burst out laughing.

"Here," they cried, "may the ice soon melt."

They started to rise, and Tash got as far as the bending of his knees. Madame turned around with a hand in the hair of her dog. Presently she drank again, looking at the door.

It had swung open and the face of Tom Scarlett peered between the jamb and the outer edge. Tash sat down.

There was something in the eye of Tom Scarlett today that they had not exactly expected to see. It was not the eye of an obscure celebrity like Tom.

He picked up an apple and bit into it.

"Ha!" he said, and once again, "Ha!" Then he burst into sudden laughter.

"Six great-little men," he shouted, abruptly, half shutting his eyes, and added sharply: "Carrion! The earth about the flower, the hand that holds the infant's mouth shut until it knows enough to be hypocritical about its saliva—" He jerked the apple away from his mouth. He bent forward until his long bathrobe touched the floor. Then his fine yellow teeth showed between his lips, held up a trifle crookedly, as a portière upon a resplendent yet gloomy room.

"What are you now?" he demanded. "Sparrows— seaweed. No, no! Hold! Businessmen. Little, dirty, gravy-spilling bourgeoisie! Hereafter you will find it difficult to swallow your bird seed."

He laughed again, sitting down among them. "Yah!" he cried, more gently. "A great man among men, that helped you to be something, but what will happen to your stature if I become a little man among little men?"

"Now what have you done?"

"I am growing my own flowers. I, too, am eating bird seed with the sparrows."

He put a handful of apple pips upon the table.

"I think I shall open a little piggery also. I shall twitter."

But tears bulged out his eyes.

SPILLWAY

Behind two spanking horses, in the heat of noon, rode Julie Anspacher. The air was full of the sound of windlasses and well water, and full too of the perfumed spindrift of flowers, and Julie stared as the road turned into the remembered distance.

The driver, an old Scandinavian and a friend of the family, who knew exactly two folk tales, one having to do with a partridge, the other with a woman, sat stiffly on his box, holding the reins slack over the sleek-rumpled mares; he was whistling the score of the story about the partridge, rocking slowly on his sturdy base, and drifting back with the tune came the strong herb-like odor of hide, smarting under straining leather.

The horses began ascending the hill, moving their ears, racking down their necks. Reaching the ridge, they bounded forward in a whirl of sparks and dust. The driver, still rigid, still whistling, taking in rein in a last flourish, raised the whipstock high in the air, setting it smartly into its socket. In a deep-pitched voice he said, "It's some time since we have seen you, Mrs. Anspacher."

Julie raised her long face from her collar and nodded.

"Yes," she said shortly, and frowned.

"Your husband has gathered in the corn already, and the orchards are hanging heavy."

"Are they?" She tried to recall how many trees were of apple and pear.

The driver changed hands on the reins, turned around: "It's good to see you again, Mrs. Anspacher." He said it so simply, with such hearty pleasure, that Julie laughed outright.

"Is it," she answered, then checked herself, fixing her angry eyes straight ahead.

The child sitting at her side, loose limbed from excessive youth, lifted her face up, on which a small aquiline nose perched with comic boldness. She half held, half dropped an old-fashioned ermine muff, the tails of which stuck out in all directions. She looked excited.

"You remember Mrs. Berling?" the driver went on. "She married again."

"Did she?"

"Yes, ma'am, she did."

He began to tell her of a vacancy in the office for outgoing mails, taken by her husband's nephew.

"Corruption!" she snorted.

The child started, then looked quickly away as children do when they expect something and do not understand what. The driver brought the whip down on the horses, left and right; a line of froth appeared along the edges of the trappings.

"You were saying, Mrs. Anspacher?"

"I was saying nothing. I said, all is lost from the beginning, if we only knew it—always."

The child looked up at her, then down into her muff.

"Ann," said Julie Anspacher suddenly, lifting the muff away from the child. "Did you ever see such big horses before?"

The child turned her head with brightness and bending down tried to see between the driver's arms.

"Are they yours?" she whispered.

"You don't have to whisper," Julie said. She took a deep breath, stretching the silk of her shirtwaist across her breasts. "And no, they are not mine, but we have two—bigger—blacker—"

"Can I see them?"

"Of course you will see them—don't be ridiculous!"

The child shrank into herself, clutching nervously at her muff. Julie Anspacher returned to her reflections.

It was almost five years since Mrs. Anspacher had been home. Five years before, in just such an autumn, the doctors had given her six months to live . . . one lung gone, the other going. They sometimes call it the "white death," sometimes the "love disease." She coughed a little, remembering, and the child at her side coughed too, as if in echo. The driver, puckering his forehead, reflected that Mrs. Anspacher was not cured.

She was thirty-nine; she should have died at thirty-four. In those five years of grace her husband Paytor had seen her five times, coming in over fourteen hours of rail, at

Christmastide. He cursed the doctors, called them fools, and each time asked her when she was coming home.

The house appeared, dull white against locust trees. Smoke, the lazy smoke that rises in the autumn in a straight column, rose up into an empty sky as the driver pulled the horses in, their foaming jaws gagging at the bit. Julie Anspacher jumped the side of the carriage at a bound, the short modish tails of her jacket dancing above her hips. She turned around, thrusting her black gloved hands under the child, lifting her to the path. A dog barked somewhere as they turned in at the gate.

A maid in a dust-cap put her head out of a window, clucked, drew it in and slammed the sash. Paytor, with slow, deliberate steps, moved across the gravel toward his wife and the child.

He was a man of middle height with a close-cropped beard that ended in a grey wedge on his chin. He was sturdy, pompous, and walked with his knees out, giving him a rocking, dependable gait; he had grave eyes and a firm mouth. He was slightly surprised. He raised the apricot-colored veil that hid Julie's face, and leaning, kissed her on both cheeks.

"And where does the child come from?" he inquired, touching the little girl's chin.

"Come along, don't be ridiculous," Julie said impatiently, and swept on toward the house.

He hurried after her. "I am so glad to see you," he said, trying to keep up with her long swinging stride, that all but lifted the child off her feet in a trotting stumble.

"Tell me what the doctors said—cured?"

There was happiness in his voice as he went on: "Not that I really care *what* they think—I always predicted a ripe old age for you, didn't I? What were the doctors' methods in regard to Marie Bashkirtseff, I ask you? They locked her up in a dark room with all the windows shut—and so of course she died—that was the method then; now it's Koch's tuberculin—and that's all nonsense too. It's good fresh air does the trick."

"It has worked for some people," she said, going ahead of him into the living room. "There was one boy there—well, of that—later. Will you have someone put Ann to bed—the trip was hard for her—see how sleepy she is. Run along, Ann," she added, pushing her slightly but gently toward the maid. When they disappeared, she stood looking about her, taking off her hat.

"I'm glad you took down the crystals—I always hated crystals—" She moved to the window.

"I didn't, the roof fell in—just after my last visit to you in December. You're looking splendid, Julie." He colored. "I'm so pleased, glad you know, awfully glad. I was beginning to think—well, not that doctors *know* anything—but it has been so long—" He tried to laugh, thought better of it, and stammered into, "It's a drop here of about fifteen hundred feet—but your heart—that is good—it always was."

"What do you know about my heart?" Julie said angrily. "You don't know what you are talking about. Now the child—"

"Yes, well?"

"Her name is Ann," she finished sulkily.

"A sweet name—it was your mother's. Whose is she?"

"Oh, good heavens!" Julie cried, moving around the room on the far side of the furniture. "Mine, mine, mine, of course! Whose would she be if not mine?"

He looked at her. "Yours? Why, Julie, how absurd!" All the color had drained from his face.

"I know—we've got to talk it over—it's all got to be arranged, it's terrible; but she is nice, a bright child, a good child."

"What in the world is all this about?" he demanded, stopping in front of her. "What are you in this mood for— what have I done?"

"Good heavens, what have *you* done! What a ridiculous man you are. Nothing, of course, absolutely nothing!" She waved her arm. "That's not it; why do you bring yourself in? I'm not blaming you, I'm not asking to be forgiven. I've been on my knees, I've beaten my head against the ground, I've abased myself, but—" she added in a terrible voice, "it's not low enough, the ground is not low enough; to bend down is not enough, to beg forgiveness is not enough; to receive?—it would not be enough. There just isn't the right kind of misery in the world for me to suffer, nor the right kind of pity for you to feel; there isn't a word in the world to heal me; penance cannot undo me—it is a thing beyond the end of everything—it's suffering without a consummation, it's like insufficient sleep; it's like anything that is without proportion. I am not asking for anything at all, because there is nothing that can be given or got—how primitive to be able to receive—"

"But, Julie—"

"No, no, it's not that," she said roughly, tears swimming in her eyes, "of course I love you. But think of this: me, a danger to everyone—excepting those like myself—in the same sickness, and expecting to die: fearful, completely involved in a problem affecting a handful of humanity—filled with fever and lust—not a self-willed lust at all, a matter of heat. And frightened, frightened! And nothing coming after, no matter what you do, nothing at all, nothing at all but death—and one goes on—it goes on—then the child—and life, hers, probably, for a time—"

"*So.*"

"So I couldn't tell you. I thought, I'll die next month, no one will ever see anything of any of us in no time now. Still, all in all, and say what I like, I didn't want to go—and I *did*—well, you know what I mean. Then her father died—they say her lungs are weak—death perpetuating itself—queer, isn't it—and the doctors—" She swung around: "You're right, they lied to me, and I lived through—all the way."

He had turned away from her.

"The real, the proper idea is," she said in a pained voice, "—is design, a thing should make a design; torment should have some meaning. I did not want to go beyond you, or to have anything beyond you—that was not the idea, not the idea at all. I thought there was to be no more me. I wanted to leave nothing behind but you, only you. You must believe this or I can't bear it . . . and still," she continued, walking around the room impatiently, "there was a sort of hysterical joy in it too. I thought, if Paytor has perception, that strange other 'something,' that must be at the center of everything (or there wouldn't be such a passionate desire for it), that something secret that is so near that it is all but obscene—well, I thought, if Paytor has this knowledge, (and mind you, I knew all the time that you didn't have it), this 'grace,' I thought, well, then he will understand. Then at such times I would say to myself, after you had been gone a long time, *now* he has the answer, at this very moment, at precisely ten-thirty of the clock, if I could be with him *now*, he would say to me, 'I see.' But as soon as I had the timetable in my hand, to look up the train you would be on; I knew there was no such feeling in your heart—nothing at all."

"Don't you feel horror?" he asked in a loud voice.

"No, I don't feel horror—horror must include conflict, and I have none; I am alien to life, I am lost in still water."

"Have you a religion, Julie?" he asked her, in the same loud voice, as if he were addressing someone a long way off.

"I don't know, I think so, but I am not sure. I've tried to believe in something external and enveloping, to carry me away, beyond—that's what we demand of our faiths, isn't it? It won't do, I lose it; I come back again to the idea that there is something more fitting than release."

He put his head in his hands. "You know," he said "I've always thought that a woman, because she *can* have children, ought to know everything. The very fact that a woman can do so preposterous a thing as have a child, ought to give her prophecy."

She coughed, her handkerchief before her face. "One learns to be careful about death, but never, never about . . ." She didn't finish but stared straight before her.

"Why did you bring the child here, why did you return at all then, after so long a time?—it's so dreadfully mixed up."

"I don't know. Perhaps because there is a right and a wrong, a good and an evil, and I had to find out. If there is such a thing as 'everlasting mercy,' I wanted to find out about that. There's such an unfamiliar taste to Christian mercy, an alien sort of intimacy . . ." She had a way of lifting the side of her face, closing her eyes. "I thought, Paytor may know—"

"Know what?"

"Division. I thought, he will be able to divide me against myself. Personally, I don't feel divided; I seem to be a sane and balanced whole, but hopelessly estranged. So I said to myself, Paytor will see where the design divides and departs, though all the time I was making no bargain, I wasn't thinking of any system—well, in other words, I wanted to be set *wrong*. Do you understand?"

"No," he said in the same loud voice, "and what's more, you yourself must know what you have done to me. You have turned everything upside down. Oh, I won't say you betrayed me—it's much less than that, and more, it's what most of us do, we betray circumstances, we don't hold on. Well," he said sharply, "I can't do anything for you, I can't do anything at all; I'm sorry, I'm very sorry, but there it is." He was grimacing and twitching his shoulders.

"The child has it too," Julie Anspacher said, looking up at him. "I shall die soon. It's ridiculous," she added, the tears streaming down her face. "You are strong, you always were, and so was your family before you—not one of them in their graves before ninety—it's all wrong—it's quite ridiculous!"

"I don't know, perhaps it's not ridiculous; one must be careful not to come too hastily to a conclusion." He began searching for his pipe. "Only you must know yourself, Julie, how I torment myself, if it's a big enough thing, for days, years. Why? Because I come to conclusions instantly and then have to fight to destroy them!" He seemed a little pompous now. "You see," he added, "I'm human, but frugal. Perhaps I'll be able to tell you something later—give you a beginning at least. Later." He turned, holding his pipe in the cup of his hand, and left the room, closing the door behind him. She heard him climbing the stairs, the hard oak steps that went up into the shooting loft, where he practiced aim at the concentric circles of his targets.

Darkness was closing in, it was eating away the bushes and the barn, and it rolled in the odors of the orchard. Julie leaned on her hand by the casement edge and listened. She could hear far off the faint sound of dogs, the brook running down the mountain, and she thought, "Water in the hand has no voice, but it really roars coming over the falls. It sings over small stones in brooks, but it only tastes of water when it's caught, struggling and running away in the hands." Tears came into her eyes, but they did not fall. Sentimental memories of childhood, she said to herself, which had sometimes been fearful, and had strong connections with fishing and skating, and the day they had made her kiss the cheek of their dead priest—*Qui habitare facit sterilem—matrem filiorum laetantem*—then *Gloria*

Patri—that had made her cry with a strange backward grief that was swallowed, because in touching his cheek, she kissed aggressive passivity, entire and cold.

She wondered and wandered in her mind. She could hear Paytor walking on the thin boards above, she could smell the smoke of his tobacco, she could hear him slashing the cocks of his guns.

Mechanically she went over to the chest in the corner; it was decorated with snow scenes. She lifted the lid. She turned over the upper layer of old laces and shawls until she came to a shirtwaist of striped silk . . . the one she had worn years ago, it had been her mother's. She stopped. The child? Paytor didn't seem to like the child. "Ridiculous!" she said out loud. "She is quiet, good, gentle. What more does he want? But no, that wasn't enough now." She removed her gloves (why hadn't she done that at once?) Perhaps she had made a mistake in coming back. Paytor was strong, all his family had been strong like that before him, and she was ill and coughing. And Ann? She had made a mistake in coming back. She went toward the stairs to call Paytor and tell him about it, pinning up her veil as she went. Time drew out. But no, that wasn't the answer, that wasn't the right idea.

The pendulum of the wooden clock, on the mantel above the fireplace, pulled time back and forth with heavy ease, and Julie, now at the window, nodded without sleep—long grotesque dreams came up to her, held themselves against her, dispersed and rolled in again. Somewhere Ann coughed in her sleep (she must be in the guest room); Julie Anspacher coughed also, holding her handkerchief to her face. She could hear feet walking back and forth, back and forth, and the smell of tobacco growing less faint.

What could she do, for God's sake, what was there that she could do? If only she had not this habit of fighting death. She shook her head. Death was past knowing, and one must be certain of something else first. "If only I had the power to feel what I should feel, but I've stood so much so long, there is not too long, that's the tragedy . . . the interminable discipline of learning to stand everything." She thought, "If only Paytor will give me time, I'll get around to it." Then it seemed that something must happen. "If only I could think of the right word before it happens," she said to herself. She said it over. "Because I am cold, I can't think. I'll think soon. I'll take my jacket off, put on my coat . . ."

She got up, running her hand along the wall. Where was it? Had she left it on the chair? "I can't think of the word," she said, to keep her mind on something.

She turned around. All his family . . . long lives . . . "and me too, me too," she murmured. She became dizzy. "It's because I must get on my knees. But it isn't low enough," she contradicted herself, "but if I put my head down, way down—down, down, down, down . . ."

She heard a shot. "He has quick warm blood—"

Her forehead had not quite touched the boards, now it touched them, but she got up immediately, stumbling over her dress.

INDIAN SUMMER

At the age of fifty-three Madame Boliver was young again. She was suddenly swept away in a mad current of reckless and beautiful youth. What she had done with those years that had counted up into such a perfect con-clusion, she could not tell—it was a strange, vague dream. She had been plain, almost ugly, shy, an old maid. She was tall and awkward—she sat down as if she were going to break when she was in those new years that girls call early bloom.

When she was thirty, she had been frankly and aston-ishingly Yankee; she came toward one with an erect and angular stride. She was severe, silent and curious. It was probably due to this that she was called Madame. She dressed in black outlined with white collar and cuffs, her hair was drawn straight back and showed large-lobed and pale ears. The tight-drawn hair exposed her features to that utter and unlovely nakedness that some clean rooms are exposed to by the catching back of heavy and melan-choly curtains—she looked out upon life with that same unaccustomed and expectant expression that best rooms wear when thrown open for the one yearly festivity that proclaims their owners well to do.

She had no friends and could not keep acquaintances— her speech was sharp, quick and truthful. She spoke seldom, but with such fierce strictness and accuracy that those who came into contact with her once, took precautions not to be thus exposed a second time.

She grew older steadily and without regret—long before the age of thirty she had given up all expectations of a usual life or any hopes of that called "unusual"; she walked in a straight path between the two, and she was content and speculated little upon this thing in her that had made her unloved and unlovely.

Her sisters had married and fallen away about her as blossoms are carried off, leaving the stalk—their children came like bits of pollen, and she enjoyed them and was mildly happy. Once she, too, had dreamed of love, but that was before she had attained to the age of seventeen—by that time she knew that no one could or would ask for her hand—she was plain and unattractive, and she was satisfied.

She had become at once the drudge and the adviser— all things were laid upon her both to solve and to produce. She labored for others easily and willingly and they let her labor.

At fifty-three she blazed into a riotous Indian Summer of loveliness. She was tall and magnificent. She carried with her a flavor of some exotic flower; she exhaled something that savored of those excellences of odor and tone akin to pain and to pleasure; she lent a plastic embodiment to all hitherto unembodied things. She was like some rare wood, carved into a melting form—she breathed abruptly as one who has been dead for half a century.

Her face, it is true, was not that plump, downy and senseless countenance of the early young—it was thin and dark and marked with a few very sensitive wrinkles; about the mouth there were signs of a humor she had never possessed, of a love she had never known, of a joy she had never experienced and of a wisdom impossible for her to have acquired. Her still, curious eyes with their blue-white borders and the splendid irises were half veiled by strange dusty lids. The hair, that had once been drawn back, was still drawn back, but no appallingly severe features were laid bare. Instead, the hair seemed to confer a favor on all those who might look upon its restrained luxury, for it uncovered a face at once valuable and unusual.

Her smile was rich in color—the scarlet of her gums, the strange whiteness of her teeth, the moisture of the sensitive mouth, all seemed as if Madame Boliver were something dyed through with perfect and rare life.

Now when she entered a room everyone paused, looking up and speaking together. She was quite conscious of this, and it pleased her—not because she was too unutterably vain, but because it was so new and so unexpected.

For a while her very youth satisfied her—she lived with herself as though she were a second person who had been permitted access to the presence of some lovely and some longed-for dream.

She did not know what to do. If she could have found religion newly with her new youth, she would have worshipped and have been profoundly glad of the kneeling down and the rising up attendant with faith, but this was a part of her old childhood and it did not serve.

She had prayed then because she was ugly; she could not pray now because she was beautiful—she wanted something new to stand before, to speak to.

One by one the old and awkward things went, leaving in their wake Venetian glass and bowls of onyx, silks, cushions and perfume. Her books became magazines with quaint, unsurpassable and daring illustrations.

Presently she had a salon. She was the rage. Gentlemen in political whiskers, pomaded and curled, left their coats in the embrace of pompous and refined footmen.

Young students with boutonnières and ambitions came; an emissary or two dropped in, proffered their hearts and departed. Poets and musicians, littèrateurs and artists experimenting in the modern, grouped themselves about her mantels like butterflies over bonbons and poured sentiment upon sentiment into her ears.

Several gentlemen of leisure and millions courted her furiously with small tears in the corners of their alert eyes. Middle-aged professors and one deacon were among the crowd that filled her handsome apartment on those days when she entertained.

There was something about Madame Boliver that could not quite succumb to herself. She was still afraid; she would start, draw her hand away and pale abruptly in the middle of some ardent proposal—she would hurry to the mirror at such times, though she never turned her head to look in.

Was it possible that she was beautiful now? And if so, would it remain? And her heart said, "Yes, it will remain," until at last she believed it.

She put the past behind her and tried to forget it. It hurt her to remember it, as if it were something that she had done in a moment of absent-mindedness and of which she had to be ashamed. She remembered it as one remembers some small wrong deed hidden for years. She thought about her past unattractiveness as another would have thought of some cruelty. Her eyes watered when she remembered her way of looking at herself in her twenties. Her mouth trembled when she thought back to its severity and its sharp retorts.

Her very body reproached her for all that had been forced upon it in her other youth, and a strange passion came upon her, turning her memory of her sisters into something at times like that hatred felt by the oppressed who remember the oppression when it has given way to plenty.

But now she was free. She expanded, she sang, she dreamed for long hours, her elbows upon the casement, looking out into the garden. She smiled, remembering the old custom of serenading, and wondered when she, too, would know it.

That she was fifty-three never troubled her. It never even occurred to her. She had been fifty-three long ago at twenty, and now she was twenty at fifty-three, that was all—this was compensation, and if she had been through her middle age in youth she could go through her youth in middle age.

At times she thought how much more beautiful nature is in its treacheries than its remedies.

Those who hovered about her offered, time on time, to marry her, to carry her away into Italy or to Spain, to lavish money and devotion on her, and in the beginning, she had been almost too ready to accept them in their assurances, because the very assurances were so new and so delightful.

But in spite of it she was, somewhere beneath her youth, old enough to know that she did not love as she would love, and she waited with a patience made pleasant by the constant attentions of the multitude.

And then Petkoff, "the Russian," had come, accompanied by one of the younger students.

A heavy fur cap came down to the borders of his squinting and piercing eyes. He wore a mixture of clothing that proclaimed him at once foreign and poor. His small mustache barely covered sensitive and well-shaped lips, and the little line of hair that reached down on each side of his close-set ears gave him an early period expression as if he, too, in spite of his few years, might have lived in the time when she was a girl.

He could not have been much over thirty, perhaps just thirty—he said little but never took his eyes off the object of his interest.

He spoke well enough, with an occasional lapse into Russian, which was very piquant. He swept aside all other aspirants with his steady and centered gaze. He ignored the rest of the company so completely as to rob him of rudeness. If one is ignorant of the very presence of his fellow beings, at most he can only be called "strange."

Petkoff was both an ambitious and a self-centered man—all his qualities were decisive and not hesitatingly crooked, providing he needed crookedness to win his point. He was attractive to Madame Boliver because he was as strange as she was herself, her youth was foreign, and so was Petkoff.

He had come to this country to start a venture that promised to be successful; in the meantime, he had to be careful both in person and in heart.

What he felt for Madame Boliver was at first astonishment that such a woman was still unmarried; he knew nothing of her past and guessed at her age much below the real figure. After a while this astonishment gave way to pleasure and then to real and very sincere love.

He began to pay court to her, neglecting his business a little and worrying over that end of it, but persisting, nevertheless.

He could see that she, on her side, was becoming deeply attached to him. He would walk about in the park for hours arguing this affair out to himself. Both the shoulds and should nots.

It got him nowhere except into a state of impatience. He liked clear-cut acts, and he could not decide to go or stay. As it was, nothing could be worse for his business than this same feverish indecision. He made up his mind.

Madame Boliver was radiantly happy. She began to draw away from a life of entertainment and, instead, turned most of her energies into the adoration of her first real love. She accepted him promptly, and with a touch of her old firm and sharp decisiveness, and a hint of her utter frankness. He told her that she took him as she would have taken a piece of cake at a tea party, and they both laughed.

That was in the winter. Madame Boliver was fifty-five —he never asked her how old she was and she never thought to tell him. They set the day for their wedding early in the following June.

They were profoundly happy. One by one the younger, more ardent admirers fell off, but very slowly; they turned their heads a little as they went, being both too vain and too skeptical to believe that this would last.

She still held receptions and still her rooms were flooded, but when Petkoff entered, a little better dressed but still a bit heedless of the throng, they hushed their highest hilarities and spoke of the new novels and the newest trend in art.

Petkoff had taken notice of them to that degree necessary to a man who knows what he has won, and from whom and how many. He looked upon them casually, but with a hint of well-being.

Madame Boliver grew more beautiful, more radiant, more easeful. Her movements began to resemble flowing water; she was almost too happy, too supple, too conscious of her well-being. She became arrogant, but still splendid; she became vain, but still gracious; she became accustomed to herself, but still reflective. She could be said to have bloomed at too auspicious an age; she was old enough to appreciate it, and this is a very dangerous thing.

She spent hours at the hairdresser's and the dressmaker's. Her dressing table resembled a battlefield. It supported all the armament for keeping age at a distance. She rode in the avenue in an open carriage, and smiled when the society notices mentioned her name and ran her picture.

She finally gave one the impression of being beautiful, but too conscious of it; talented, but too vain; easy of carriage, but too reliant on it; of being strange and rare and wonderful, but a little too strange, a little too rare, a little too wonderful. She became magnificently complex to outward appearances, yet in her soul Madame Boliver still kept her honesty, her frankness and her simplicity.

And then one day Madame Boliver took to her bed. It began with a headache and ended with severe chills. She hoped to get up on the following day, and she remained there a week; she put her party off, expecting to be able to be about, but instead she gave it sitting in a chair supported by cushions.

Petkoff was worried and morose. He had given a good deal of time to Madame Boliver, and he cared for her in a selfish and all-engrossing way. When she stood up no longer, he broke a Venetian tumbler by throwing it into the fireplace. When she laughed at this he suddenly burst out into very heavy weeping. She tried to comfort him, but he would not be comforted. She promised him that she would walk soon, as a mother promises a child some longed-for object. When she said, "I will be well, dear, soon; after all I'm a young woman," he stopped and looked at her through a film of painful tears.

"But are you?" he said, voicing for the first time his inner fear.

And it was then that the horror of the situation dawned upon her. In youth, when youth comes rightly, there is old age in which to lose it complacently, but when it comes in old age there is no time to watch it go.

She sat up and stared at him.

"Why, yes," she said in a flat and firm voice, "that's so. I am no longer of few years."

She could not say "no longer young," because she was young.

"It will make no difference."

"Ah," she said, "it will make no difference to you, but it will make a difference to us."

She lay back and sighed, and presently she asked him to leave her a little while.

When he had gone, she summoned the doctor.

She said: "My friend—am I dying—so soon?"

He shook his head emphatically. "Of course not," he assured her; "we will have you up in a week or so."

"What is it, then, that keeps me here now?"

"You have tired yourself out, that is all. You see, such extensive entertaining, my dear madame, will tax the youngest of us." He shook his head at this and twisted his mustache. She sent him away also.

The next few days were happy ones. She felt better. She sat up without fatigue. She was joyful in Petkoff's renewed affections. He had been frightened, and he lavished more extravagant praise and endearing terms on her than ever before. He was like a man who, seeing his fortune go, found how dear it was to him after all and how necessary when it returned to him. By almost losing her he appreciated what he should have felt if he had lost her indeed.

It got to be a joke between them that they had held any fears at all. At the club he beat his friends on the back and cried:

"Gentlemen, a beautiful and young woman." And they used to beat his back, exclaiming: "Lucky, by God!"

She ordered a large stock of wine and cakes for the wedding party, bought some new Venetian glasses and indulged in a few rare old carpets for the floor. She had quite a fancy, too, for a new gown offered at a remarkably low sum, but she began to curb herself, for she had been very extravagant as it was.

And then one day she died.

Petkoff came in a wild, strange mood. Four candles were burning at head and feet, and Madame Boliver was more lovely than ever. Stamping, so that he sent up little spirals of dust from the newly acquired carpet, Petkoff strode up and down beside the bier. He leaned over and lit a cigarette by one of the flickering flames of the candles. Madame Boliver's elderly sister, who was kneeling, coughed and looked reproachfully upward at the figure of Petkoff, who had once again forgotten everyone and everything. "Damn it!" he said, putting his fingers into his vest.

THE ROBIN'S HOUSE

In a stately decaying mansion, on the lower end of the Avenue, lived a woman by the name of Nelly Grissard.

Two heavy cocks stood on either side of the brownstone steps, looking out toward the park; and in the back garden a fountain, having poured out its soul for many a year, still poured, murmuring over the stomachs of the three cherubim supporting its massive basin.

Nelly Grissard was fat and lively to the point of excess. She never let a waxed floor pass under her without proving herself light of foot. Every ounce of Nelly Grissard was on the jump. Her fingers tapped, her feet fluttered, her bosom heaved; her entire diaphragm swelled with little creakings of whalebone, lace and taffeta.

She wore feathery things about the throat, had a liking for deep burgundy silks, and wore six petticoats for the "joy of discovering that I'm not so fat as they say." She stained her good square teeth with tobacco and cut her hair in a bang.

Nelly Grissard was fond of saying: "I'm more French than human." Her late husband had been French; had dragged his nationality about with him with the melancholy of a man who had half-dropped his cloak and that cloak his life, and in the end, having wrapped it tightly about him, had departed as a Frenchman should.

There had been many "periods" in Nelly Grissard's life: a Russian, a Greek, and those privileged to look through her keyhole said, even a Chinese.

She believed in "intuition," but it was always first-hand intuition; she learned geography by a strict system of love affairs—never two men from the same part of the country.

She also liked receiving "spirit messages"—they kept her in touch with international emotion—she kept many irons in the fire and not the least of them was the "spiritual" iron.

Then she had what she called a "healing touch"—she could take away headaches, and she could tell by one pass of her hand if the bump on that particular head was a bump of genius or of avarice—or if (and she used to shudder, closing her eyes and withdrawing her hand with a slow, poised and expectant manner) it was the bump of the senses.

Nelly was, in other words, dangerously careful of her sentimentalism. No one but a sentimental woman would have called her great roomy mansion "The Robin's House"; no one but a sentimentalist could possibly have lived through so many days and nights of saying "yes" breathlessly, or could have risen so often from her bed with such a magnificent and knowing air.

No one looking through the gratings of the basement window would have guessed at the fermenting mind of Nelly Grissard. Here well-starched domestics rustled about, laying cool fingers on cool fowls and frosted bottles. The cook, it is true, was a little untidy; he would come and stand in the entry, when spring was approaching, and look over the head of Nelly Grissard's old nurse, who sat in a wheel-chair all day, her feeble hands crossed over a discarded rug of the favorite burgundy color, staring away with half-melted eyes into the everlasting fountain, while below the cook's steaming face, on a hairy chest, rose and fell a faded holy amulet.

Sometimes the world paused to see Nelly Grissard pounce down the steps, one after another, and with a final swift and high gesture take her magnificent legs out for a drive, the coachman cracking his whip, the braided ribbons dancing at the horses' ears. And that was about all—no, if one cared to notice, a man, in the early forties, who passed every afternoon just at four, swinging a heavy black cane.

This man was Nicholas Golwein—half Tartar, half Jew.

There was something dark, evil and obscure about Nicholas Golwein, and something bending, kindly, compassionate. Yet he was a very Jew by nature. He rode little, danced less, but smoked great self-reassuring cigars, and could out-ponder the average fidgety American by hours.

He had traveled, he had lived as the "Romans lived," and had sent many a hot-eyed girl back across the fields with something to forget or remember, according to her nature.

This man had been Nelly Grissard's lover at the most depraved period of Nelly's life. At that moment when she was coloring her drinking water green and living on ox liver and "testina en broda," Nicholas Golwein had turned her collar back, and kissed her on that intimate portion of the throat where it has just left daylight, yet has barely passed into the shadow of the breast.

To be sure, Nelly Grissard had been depraved at an exceedingly early age, if depravity is understood to be the ability to enjoy what others shudder at, and to shudder at what others enjoy. Nelly Grissard dreamed "absolutely honestly"—stress on the absolutely—when it was all the fashion to dream obscurely—she could sustain the conversation just long enough not to be annoyingly brilliant, she loved to talk of ancient crimes, drawing her stomach in, and bending her fingers slightly, just slightly, but also just enough to make the guests shiver a little and think how she really should have been born in the time of the Cenci. And during the craze for Gauguin, she was careful to mention that she had passed over the same South Sea roads, but where Gauguin had walked, she had been carried by two astonished donkeys.

She had been "kind" to Nicholas Golwein just long enough to make the racial melancholy blossom into a rank tall weed. He loved beautiful things, and she possessed them. He had become used to her, had "forgiven" her much (for those who had to forgive at all had to forgive Nelly in a large way), and the fact that she was too fluid to need one person's forgiveness long, drove him into slow bitterness and despair.

The fact that "her days were on her," and that she did not feel the usual woman's fear of age and dissolution, nay, that she even saw new measures to take, possessing a fertility that can only come of a decaying mind, drove him almost into insanity.

When the autumn came, and the leaves were falling from the trees, as nature grew hot and the last flames of the season licked high among the branches, Nicholas Golwein's cheeks burned with a dull red, and he turned his eyes down.

Life did not exist for Nicholas Golwein as a matter of day and after day—it was flung at him from time to time as a cloak is flung a flunkey, and this made him proud, morose, silent.

Was it not somehow indecent that, after his forgiveness and understanding, there should be the understanding and forgiveness of another?

There was undoubtedly something cruel about Nelly Grissard's love; she took at random, and Nicholas Golwein had been the most random, perhaps, of all. The others, before him, had all been of her own class—the first had even married her, and when she finally drove him to the knife's edge, had left her a fair fortune. Nicholas Golwein had always earned his own living, he was an artist and lived as artists live. Then Nelly came and went—and after him she had again taken one of her own kind, a wealthy Norwegian—Nord, a friend of Nicholas'.

Sometimes now Nicholas Golwein would go off into the country, trying to forget, trying to curb the tastes that Nelly's love had nourished. He nosed out small towns, but he always came hurriedly back, smelling of sassafras, the dull penetrating odor of grass, contact with trees, half-tamed animals.

The country made him think of Schubert's Unfinished Symphony—he would start running—running seemed a way to complete all that was sketchy and incomplete about nature, music, love.

"Would I recognize God if I saw him?" The joy of thinking such thoughts was not every man's, and this cheered him.

Sometimes he would go to see Nord; he was not above visiting Nelly's lover—in fact there was that between them.

He had fancied death lately. There was a tremendously sterile quality about Nicholas Golwein's fancies; they were the fancies of a race, and not of a man.

He discussed death with Nord—before the end there is something pleasant in a talk of a means to an end, and Nord had the coldness that makes death strong.

"I can hate," he would say, watching Nord out of the corner of his eye; "Nelly can't, she's too provincial—"

"Yes, there's truth in that. Nelly's good to herself— what more is there?"

"There's understanding." He meant compassion, and his eyes filled. "Does she ever speak of me?"

It was beginning to rain. Large drops struck softly against the café window and thinning out ran down upon the sill.

"Oh, yes."

"And she says?"

"Why are you never satisfied with what you have, Nicholas?"

Nicholas Golwein turned red. "One dish of cream and the cat should lick his paws into eternity. I suppose one would learn how she felt, if she feels at all, if one died."

"Why, yes, I suppose so."

They looked at each other, Nicholas Golwein in a furtive manner, moving his lips around his cigar—Nord absently, smiling a little. "Yes, that would amuse her."

"What?" Nicholas Golwein paused in his smoking and let his hot eyes rest on Nord.

"Well, if you can manage it—"

Nicholas Golwein made a gesture, shaking his cufflinks like a harness—"I can manage it," he said, wondering what Nord was thinking.

"Of course it's rather disgusting," Nord said.

"I know, I know I should go out like a gentleman, but there's more in me than the gentleman, there's something that understands meanness; a Jew can only love and be intimate with the thing that's a little abnormal, and so I love what's low and treacherous and cunning, because there's nobility and uneasiness in it for me—well," he flung out his arms—"if you were to say to Nell, 'He hung himself in the small hours, with a sheet'—what then? Everything she had ever said to me, been to me, will change for her—she won't be able to read those French journals in the same way, she won't be able to swallow water as she has always swallowed it. I know, you'll say there's nature and do you know what I'll answer: that I have a contempt for animals—just because they do not have to include Nelly Grissard's whims in their means to a living conduct—well, listen, I've made up my mind to something"—he became calm all of a sudden and looked Nord directly in the face.

"Well?"

"I shall follow you up the stairs, stand behind the door, and you shall say just these words, 'Nicholas has hung himself.'"

"And then what?"

"That's all, that's quite sufficient—then I shall know everything."

Nord stood up, letting Nicholas open the café door for him.

"You don't object?" Nicholas Golwein murmured.

Nord laughed a cold, insulting laugh. "It will amuse her—"

Nicholas nodded, "Yes, we've held the coarse essentials between our teeth like good dogs—" he said, trying to be insulting in turn, but it only sounded pathetic, sentimental.

Without a word passing between them, on the following day, they went up the stairs of Nelly Grissard's house, together. The door into the inner room was ajar, and Nicholas crept in behind this, seating himself on a little table.

He heard Nord greet Nelly, and Nelly's voice answering— "Ah, dear"—he listened no further for a moment, his mind went back, and he seemed to himself to be peaceful and happy all at once. "A binding up of old sores," he thought, a oneness with what was good and simple—with everything that evil had not contorted.

"Religion," he thought to himself, resting his chin on his hands—thinking what religion had meant to all men at all times, but to no man in his most need. "Religion is a design for pain—that's it." Then he thought, that, like all art, must be fundamentally against God—God had made his own plans—well, of that later—

Nelly had just said something—there had been a death-like silence, then her cry, but he had forgotten to listen to what it was that had passed. He changed hands on his cane. "There is someone in heaven," he found his mind saying. The rising of this feeling was pleasant—it seemed to come from the very center of his being. "There's someone in heaven—who?" he asked himself, "who?" But there was no possible answer that was not blasphemy.

"Jews do not kill themselves—"

Nelly's voice. He smiled—there was someone in heaven, but no one here. "I'm coming," he murmured to himself—and felt a sensuous going away in the promise.

His eyes filled. What was good in death had been used up long ago—now it was only dull repetition—death had gone beyond the need of death.

Funnily enough he thought of Nelly as she was that evening when she had something to forgive. He had pulled her toward him by one end of a burgundy ribbon, "Forgive, forgive," and she had been kind enough not to raise him, not to kiss him, saying, "I forgive"—she just stood there showing her tobacco-stained teeth in a strong laugh, "Judas eliminated." He put his hand to his mouth, "I have been *There*," and *There* seemed like a place where no one had ever been. How cruel, how monstrous!

Someone was running around the room, heavy, ponderous. "She always prided herself on her lightness of foot," and here she was running like a trapped animal, making little cries, "By the neck!"—strange words, horrifying, unreal—

"To be a little meaner than the others, a little more crafty"—well, he had accomplished that, too.

Someone must be leaning on the couch, it groaned. That took him back to Boulogne; he had loved a girl once in Boulogne, and once in the dark they had fallen—it was like falling through the sky, through the stars, finding that the stars were not only one layer thick, but that there were many layers, millions of layers, a thickness to them, and a depth—then the floor—that was like a final promise of something sordid, but lasting—firm.

Sounds rose from the streets; automobiles going up town, horses' hoofs, a cycle siren—that must be a child—long drawn out, and piercing—yes, only a child would hold on to a sound like that.

"Life is life," Nelly had just said, firmly, decisively. After all he had done this well—he had never been able to think of death long, but now he had thought of it, made it pretty real—he remembered sparrows, for some unknown reason, and this worried him. "The line of the hips, simply Renoir over again—"

They were on the familiar subject of art.

The sounds in the room twittered about him like wings in a close garden, where there is neither night nor day. "There is a power in death, even the thought of death, that is very terrible and very beautiful—" His cane slipped and struck the floor.

"What was that?" the voice of Nelly Grissard was high, excited, startled—

"A joke."

Nicholas Golwein suddenly walked into the room.

"A joke," he said and looked at them both, smiling.

Nelly Grissard, who was on her knees, and who was holding Nord's shoe in one hand, stared at him. It seemed that she must have been about to kiss Nord's foot.

Nicholas Golwein bowed, a magnificent bow, and was about to go.

"You ought to be ashamed of yourself," Nelly Grissard cried, angrily, and got to her feet.

He began to stammer: "I—I am leaving town—I wanted to pay my respects—"

"Well, go along with you—"

Nicholas Golwein went out, shutting the door carefully behind him.

THE PASSION

Every afternoon at four-thirty, excepting Thursday, a smart carriage moved with measured excellence through the Bois, drawn by two bays in shining patent leather blinkers, embellished with silver R's, the docked tails rising proudly above well-stitched immaculate cruppers.

In this carriage, with its half-closed curtains, sat the Princess Frederica Rholinghausen, erect, in the dead center of a medallioned cushion.

Behind the tight-drawn veiling that webbed the flaring brim of a Leghorn hat burdened with ribbons and roses, the imperturbable face was no longer rouged to heighten contour, but to limn a noble emaciation. The tall figure, with its shoulders like delicate flying buttresses, was encased in grey moiré, the knees dropping the stiff excess in two sharp points, like the corners of a candy box. No pearl in the dog-collar shook between the dipping blue of the veins, nor did the radiance on the finger-nails shift by any personal movement; the whole glitter of the jeweled bones and the piercing eye, turned with the turning of the coach, as it passed the lake with creaking waterfowl, and rolled free from the trapping shadow of branchless boles.

The coachman, sitting up on the box with his son, was breaking the young man in for a life of driving, in which the old man would have no part. On every Thursday, when the princess was at home, the empty carriage was driven at a smart rocking pace, and every Thursday the Allée de Longchamp rang with the old man's shouts of *"Eh, doucement, doucement!"*

The family retainers, now only five, worked with as little effort as was compatible with a slowing routine. Every morning the books in the library, with their white kid bindings and faded coat of arms, were dusted, and every afternoon, when the sun wasn't too blazing, the curtains in the conservatoire were drawn back, but as the princess moved from room to room less every year, one chamber was closed for good every twelvemonth.

In the kitchen, regular as the clock, the cook whipped up the whites of three eggs, with rum and sugar, for the evening *soufflé*; and just as regularly, the gardener watered the plants at nightfall, as though promoted, for in the still splendor of the château gardens, one drank the dark cumbersome majesty as of Versailles.

The lapdog, long since too old to lift from her basket of ruffled chintz, slept heavily, a mass of white fur, unmarked of limb, or feature, save for the line of dark hair that placed the eyelids, and the moist down-drooping point below the chin.

On her Thursdays the princess arose at three, dressing herself before a long oak stand, blazing with faceted bottles. She had been nearly six feet tall; now she had waned but little under it. There were cut flowers where she went, but she did not tend them. The scenes of the chase, hanging on the wall between the tall oak chairs, were feathered with dust and out of mind. She had painted them when she was young. The spinet in the corner, covered with a yellow satin throw, embroidered by her own hand, was crumbling along the bevel of the lid, signifying silence of half a century. The scores, lying one above the other, were for soprano. One was open at *Liebes-lied*. The only objects to have seen recent service were the candelabrum, the candles, half burnt upon their spikes, for the princess read into the night.

There were only two portraits, they were in the dining hall; one, her father, in uniform, standing beside a table, his plumed hat in his hand, his hand on the hilt of a sword, his spurred heels lost in the deep pile of a rug. The other, her mother, seated on a garden bench, dressed in hunter green, a little mannish hat tilted to one side. In one fist she held a cascade of ruffles above high riding-boots. A baroque case held miniatures of brothers and cousins; rosy-cheeked, moon-haired, sexless children smiling among the bric-à-brac; fans, coins, seals, porcelain platters (fired with eagles), and, incongruously, a statuette of a lady looking down through the film of her nightshift at her colorless breasts.

Sometimes it rained, splashing drops on the long French windows, the reflection stormed in the mirrors. Sometimes the sun struck a crystal, which in turn flung a cold wing of fire upon the ceiling.

In short, the princess was very old. Now it is said that the old cannot approach the grave without fearful apprehension or religious rite. The princess did. She was in the hand of a high decay: she was *sèche*, but living on the last suppuration of her will.

Sometimes, not often, but sometimes she laughed, with the heartiness of something remembered inappropriately, and laughter in an ancient is troubling, because inclement and isolated. At times, raising her eyeglasses at the uncompromising moment, she had surprisingly, the air of a *galant*, a *bon-vivant*—but there was a wash of blue in her flesh that spoke of the acceptance of mortality. She never spoke of the spirit.

Now and again two rusty female aunts called, accompanied by tottering companions, equally palsied and broken, who nevertheless managed to retrieve fallen objects, mislaid spectacles, and crumbled cake—patiently bending and unbending, their breast watches swinging from silver hooks.

Sometimes an only nephew, a "scamp," not too childish in his accomplishments, impudent and self-absolved, strolled in—after stabling his horse—walking with legs well apart, slapping his puttees with the loop of his crop, swaggering the length of the room, promising "deathless devotion," holding out, at arm's length, a sturdy zinnia. Then collapsing into a chair (with the ease of inherited impudence, in courtly femur and fibula, in unhampered bone and unearned increment) he sipped at the frail teacup and, biting wide crescents in the thin buttered bread, stared out into the fields with a cold and calculating eye; and when the princess left the room, he really didn't care.

Kurt Anders, a Polish officer, of some vaguely remembered regiment, who almost never appeared in uniform, was the chiefess among her callers. Once a month, on the second Thursday, for some thirty years, he had presented himself, drinking delicately from the same china as though he were not a giant, well trussed and top heavy. Two long folds spread away from the long dipping hooked nose under which his mouth, too small and flat for the wide teeth, pursued the cup. He spoke with a marked accent.

He was a widower. He collected plate and early editions, firearms and stamps. He was devoted to the seventeenth century. He wore puce gloves which, when he rolled them down in one true stroke, sent a faint odor of violet into the room. He had the bearing of one who had abetted license, he looked as though he had eaten everything: but though elegant in his person, there was something about him not far from the stool.

Sometimes calling a little early, he would go off to the stables where the two bays, now the only horses, stamped and were curried, and where a pleasing brawl of bitches, weighed down with the season's puppies, fawned and snapped. Anders would stoop to stroke their muzzles, pulling at their leather collars, pausing long enough to balance their tails.

This man, whose history was said to have been both *éblouissant* and dark, and who, the gossips said, had most certainly disappointed his family in youth, was, without doubt, a figure of *scandale*. He had been much too fond of the *demi-monde*. He enjoyed any great man's "favorite." He had a taste for all who would have to be "forgiven." He had been much in the company of a "darling" of the academy, scion of the house of Valois, the one they called "L'Infidèle"—or so he said—who, though passionately "modern" could not keep away from museum or waxwork (particularly the roped-off sections housing royal equipages, or the presently historically safe beds of lost kings) and who, on one or more occasion, had been seen to wipe the corner of his eye with a fine pocket handkerchief.

The truth? Anders enjoyed the maneuvre, the perfected "leap," the trick pulled off. Imposing, high stomached, spatted, gloved, he strolled the Luxembourg, watching the leaves falling on the statues of dead queens, the toy boats on the pond, the bows bobbing on the backsides of little girls, the people sitting and saying nothing. If one is some day to enjoy paradise? Then the one irreparable loss is any park in Paris that one can no longer visit.

Later, coming into the music-room, stripping off his gloves, he would speak of the dogs, of the races, of the autumn, of the air in relation to the autumn and the air of other countries; he would speak in praise of this or that cathedral, this or that drama. Sometimes he set up before the princess a rare etching that he hoped she would like, or he would walk up and down before her until she noticed the pockets of his coat, into which he had stuck small flowers. Sometimes he forgot horses and dogs, etchings and autumns, and would concentrate on the use and the decline of the rapier, and of the merit of the high boot for the actor. The princess would quote Schiller. Then Anders would plunge into the uses of the fool in Shakespeare, turning and turning a thin gold band on his little finger (winking with a ruby as tender as water), weighing a point the princess had made, regarding the impracticability of maintaining tradition, now that every man was his own fool. They might get off on to literature in general, and she would ask if he were well versed in the poetry of Britain. He would answer that Chaucer caught him and was a devil of a fellow to shake off. She would inquire gravely "Why shake?" and then drift on to a discussion of painting, and how it had left the home *genre* when the Dutch gave way to the English. They would argue for and against indoor and outdoor subjects for oils; and now and then the whole dispute would turn off to a suggested trip, to view a fine piece of Spanish furniture. Sometimes he left the etching.

Of course, everyone assumed the princess the one true passion of his life. It was taken for granted that, but for a rupture suffered in the Franco-Prussian War, he would have claimed her for bride. Others were just as certain the princess was far too niggardly to share the half of her bed. The rest insisted that they had been lovers in youth and were now as good as husband and wife.

All of this was nonsense.

They were pages in an old volume, brought together by the closing of the book.

On the last call but one, there had been something of a strain. He had mentioned Gesualdo and the sorrows of the assassin; and from the assassin to the passion of Monteverdi "at the tomb of the beloved."

"The 'walking straight up to dreadfulness,'" he said, "that is love."

He stopped directly in front of her as he spoke, leaning toward her to see how she did, and she, bent back and peering, said: "The last attendant on an old woman is always an 'incurable.'" She set her teacup down with a slight trembling of the hand, then drawing her eyeglasses up, she added with mordant acerbity, "But—if a little light man with a beard had said 'I love you,' I should have believed in God."

He called only once after that, and only once was the princess seen riding in the Bois, a mist behind a tight drawn veil. Shortly after, she did not live.

ALLER ET RETOUR

The train travelling from Marseilles to Nice had on board a woman of great strength.

She was well past forty and a little top-heavy. Her bosom was tightly cross-laced, the busk bending with every breath, and as she breathed and moved, she sounded with many chains in coarse gold links, the ring of large heavily set jewels marking off her lighter gestures. From time to time, she raised a long-handled *lorgnette* to her often winking brown eyes, surveying the countryside blurred in smoke from the train.

At Toulon, she pushed down the window, leaning out, calling for beer, the buff of her hip-fitting skirt rising in a peak above tan boots laced high on shapely legs, and above that the pink of woolen stockings. She settled back, drinking her beer with pleasure, controlling the jarring of her body with the firm pressure of her small plump feet against the rubber matting.

She was a Russian, a widow. Her name was Erling von Bartmann. She lived in Paris.

In leaving Marseilles she had purchased a copy of *Madame Bovary*, and now she held it in her hands, elbows slightly raised and out.

She read a few sentences with difficulty, then laid the book on her lap, looking at the passing hills.

Once in Marseilles, she traversed the dirty streets slowly, holding the buff skirt well above her boots, in a manner at once careful and absent. The thin skin of her nose quivered as she drew in the foul odors of the smaller passages, but she looked neither pleased nor displeased.

She went up the steep narrow littered streets abutting on the port, staring right and left, noting every object.

A gross woman, with wide set legs, sprawled in the doorway to a single room, gorged with a high-posted rusting iron bed. The woman was holding a robin loosely in one huge plucking hand. The air was full of floating feathers, falling and rising about girls with bare shoulders, blinking under coarse dark bangs. Madame von Bartmann picked her way carefully.

At a ship-chandler's she stopped, smelling the tang of tarred rope. She took down several colored postcards showing women in the act of bathing; of happy mariners leaning above full-busted sirens with sly cogged eyes. Madame von Bartmann touched the satins of vulgar, highly colored bedspreads laid out for sale in a side alley. A window, fly-specked, dusty and cracked, displayed, terrace upon terrace, white and magenta funeral wreaths, wired in beads, flanked by images of the Bleeding Heart, embossed in tin, with edgings of beaten flame, the whole beached on a surf of metal lace.

She returned to her hotel room and stood, unpinning her hat and veil before the mirror in the tall closet door.

She sat, to unlace her boots, in one of eight chairs, arranged in perfect precision along the two walls. The thick boxed velvet curtains blocked out the court where pigeons were sold. Madame von Bartmann washed her hands with a large oval of coarse red soap, drying them, trying to think.

In the morning, seated on the stout linen sheets of the bed, she planned the rest of her journey. She was two or three hours too early for her train. She dressed and went out. Finding a church, she entered and drew her gloves off slowly. It was dark and cold, and she was alone. Two small oil lamps burned on either side of the figures of St. Anthony and St. Francis. She put her leather bag on a form and went into a corner, kneeling down. She turned the stones of her rings out and put her hands together, the light shining between the little fingers; raising them she prayed, with all her vigorous understanding, to God, for a common redemption.

She got up, peering about her, angry that there were no candles burning to the *Magnifique*—feeling the stuff of the altar-cloth.

At Nice she took an omnibus, riding second class, reaching the outskirts about four. She opened the high rusty gates to a private park, with a large iron key, and closed it behind her.

The lane of flowering trees with their perfumed cups, the moss that leaded the broken paving stones, the hot musky air, the incessant rustling wings of unseen birds— all ran together in a tangle of singing textures, light and dark.

The avenue was long and without turning until it curved between two massive jars, spiked with spirals of cacti, and just behind these, the house of plaster and stone.

There were no shutters open on the avenue because of insects, and Madame von Bartmann went slowly, still holding her skirts, around to the side of the house, where a long-haired cat lay softly in the sun. Madame von Bartmann looked up at the windows, half shuttered, paused, thought better of it and struck off into the wood beyond.

The deep pervading drone of ground insects ceased about her chosen steps, and she turned her head, looking up into the occasional touches of sky.

She still held the key to the gate in her gloved hand, and the seventeen-year-old girl who came up from a bush took hold of it, walking beside her.

The child was still in short dresses, and the pink of her knees was dulled by the dust of the underbrush. Her squirrel-colored hair rose in two ridges of light along her head, descending to the lobes of her long ears, where it was caught into a faded green ribbon.

"Richter!" Madame von Bartmann said (her husband had wanted a boy).

The child put her hands behind her back before answering.

"I've been out there, in the field."

Madame von Bartmann, walking on, made no answer.

"Did you stop in Marseilles, Mother?"

She nodded.

"Long?"

"Two days and a half."

"Why a half?"

"The trains."

"Is it a big city?"

"Not very, but dirty."

"Is there anything nice there?"

Madame von Bartmann smiled: "The Bleeding Heart—sailors—"

Presently they came out into the open field, and Madame von Bartmann, turning her skirt back, sat down on a knoll, warm with tempered grass.

The child, with slight springiness of limb, due to youth, sat beside her.

"Shall you stay home now?"

"For quite a while."

"Was Paris nice?"

"Paris was Paris."

The child was checked. She began pulling at the grass. Madame von Bartmann drew off one of her tan gloves, split at the turn of the thumb, and stopped for a moment before she said: "Well, now that your father is dead—"

The child's eyes filled with tears; she lowered her head.

"I come flying back," Madame von Bartmann continued good-naturedly, "to look at my own. Let me see you," she continued, turning the child's chin up in the palm of her hand. "Ten, when I last saw you, and now you are a woman." With this she dropped the child's chin and put on her glove.

"Come," she said, rising, "I haven't seen the house in years." As they went down the dark avenue, she talked.

"Is the black marble Venus still in the hall?"

"Yes."

"Are the chairs with the carved legs still in existence?"

"Only two. Last year Erna broke one, and the year before—"

"Well?"

"I broke one."

"Growing up," Madame von Bartmann commented. "Well, well. Is the great picture still there, over the bed?"

The child, beneath her breath, said: "That's my room."

Madame von Bartmann, unfastening her *lorgnette* from its hook on her bosom, put it to her eyes and regarded the child.

"You are very thin."

"I'm growing."

"I grew, but like a pigeon. Well, one generation can't be exactly like another. You have your father's red hair. That," she said abruptly, "was a queer, mad fellow, that Herr von Bartmann. I never could see what we were doing with each other. As for you," she added, shutting her glasses, "I'll have to see what he has made of you."

In the evening, in the heavy house with its heavy furniture, Richter watched her mother, still in hat and spotted veil, playing on the sprawling lanky grand, high up behind the terrace window. It was a waltz. Madame von Bartmann played fast, with effervescence, the sparkles of her jeweled fingers bubbled over the keys.

In the dark of the garden, Richter listened to Schubert streaming down the light from the open casement. The child was cold now, and she shivered in the fur coat that touched the chill of her knees.

Still swiftly, with a *finale* somewhat in the Grand Opera manner, Madame von Bartmann closed the piano, stood a moment on the balcony inhaling the air, fingering the coarse links of her chain, the insects darting vertically across her vision.

Presently she came out and sat down on a stone bench, quietly, waiting.

Richter stood a few steps away and did not approach or speak. Madame von Bartmann began, though she could not see the child without turning:

"You have been here always, Richter?"

"Yes," the child answered.

"In this park, in this house, with Herr von Bartmann, the tutors and the dogs?"

"Yes."

"Do you speak German?"

"A little."

"Let me hear."

"Müde bin Ich, geh' zu Ruh."

"French?"

"O nuit désastreuse! O nuit effroyable!"

"Russian?"

The child did not answer.

"Ach!" said Madame von Bartmann. Then: "Have you been to Nice?"

"Oh, yes, often."

"What did you see there?"

"Everything."

Madame von Bartmann laughed. She leaned forward, her elbow on her knee, her face in her palm. The earrings in her ears stood still, the drone of the insects was clear and soft; pain lay fallow.

"Once," she said, "I was a child like you. Fatter, better health—nevertheless like you. I loved nice things. But," she added, "a different kind, I imagine. Things that were positive. I liked to go out in the evening, not because it was sweet and voluptuous—but to frighten myself, because I'd known it such a little while, and after me it would exist so long. But that—" she interrupted herself, "is beside the point. Tell me how you feel."

The child moved in the shadow. "I can't."

Madame von Bartmann laughed again but stopped abruptly.

"Life," she said, "is filthy; it is also frightful. There is everything in it: murder, pain, beauty, disease—death. Do you know this?"

The child answered, "Yes."

"How do you know?"

The child answered again, "I don't know."

"You see!" Madame von Bartmann went on, "you know nothing. You must know *everything*, and *then* begin. You must have a great understanding, or accomplish a fall. Horses hurry you away from danger; trains bring you back. Paintings give the heart a mortal pang—they hung over a man you loved and perhaps murdered in his bed. Flowers hearse up the heart because a child was buried in them. Music incites to the terror of repetition. The cross-roads are where lovers vow, and taverns are for thieves. Contemplation leads to prejudice; and beds are fields where babies fight a losing battle. Do you know all this?"

There was no answer from the dark.

"Man is rotten from the start," Madame von Bartmann continued. "Rotten with virtue and with vice. He is strangled by the two and made nothing; and God is the light the mortal insect kindled, to turn to, and to die by. That is very wise, but it must not be misunderstood. I do not want you to turn your nose up at any whore in any street;

pray and wallow and cease, but without prejudice. A murderer may have less prejudice than a saint; sometimes it is better to be a saint. Do not be vain about your indifference, should you be possessed of indifference; and don't," she said, "misconceive the value of your passions; it is only seasoning to the whole horror. I wish . . ." She did not finish, but quietly took her pocket handkerchief and silently dried her eyes.

"What?" the child asked from the darkness.

Madame von Bartmann shivered. "Are you thinking?" she said.

"No," the child answered.

"Then *think*," Madame von Bartmann said loudly, turning to the child. "Think everything, good, bad, indifferent; everything, and *do* everything, *everything*! Try to know what you are before you die. And," she said, putting her head back and swallowing with shut eyes, "come back to me a good woman."

She got up then and went away, down the long aisle of trees.

That night, at bedtime, Madame von Bartmann, rolled up in a bed with a canopy of linen roses, frilled and smelling of lavender, called through the curtains:

"Richter, do you play?"

"Yes," answered Richter.

"Play me something."

Richter heard her mother turn heavily, breathing comfort.

Touchingly, with frail legs pointed to the pedals, Richter, with a thin technique and a light touch, played something from Beethoven.

"*Brava!*" her mother called, and she played again, and this time there was silence from the canopied bed. The child closed the piano, pulling the velvet over the mahogany, put the light out and went, still shivering in her short coat, out on to the balcony.

A few days later, having avoided her mother, looking shy, frightened and offended, Richter came into her mother's room. She spoke directly and sparingly:

"Mother, with your consent, I should like to announce my engagement to Gerald Teal." Her manner was stilted. "Father approved of him. He knew him for years: if you permit—"

"Good heavens!" exclaimed Madame von Bartmann, and swung clear around on her chair. "Who is he? What is he like?"

"He is a clerk in government employ; he is young—"

"Has he money?"

"I don't know: father saw to that."

There was a look of pain and relief on Madame von Bartmann's face.

"Very well," she said, "I shall have dinner for you two at eight-thirty sharp."

At eight-thirty sharp they were dining. Madame von Bartmann, seated at the head of the table, listened to Mr. Teal speaking.

"I shall do my best to make your daughter happy. I am a man of staid habits, no longer too young," he smiled. "I have a house on the outskirts of Nice. My income is assured—a little left me by my mother. My sister is my housekeeper, she is a maiden lady, but very cheerful and very good." He paused, holding a glass of wine to the light.

"We hope to have children—Richter will be occupied. As she is delicate, we shall travel, to Vichy, once a year. I have two very fine horses and a carriage with sound springs. She will drive in the afternoons, when she is indisposed— though I hope she will find her greatest happiness at home."

Richter, sitting at her mother's right hand, did not look up.

Within two months Madame von Bartmann was once again in her travelling clothes, hatted and veiled, strapping her umbrella as she stood on the platform, waiting for the train to Paris. She shook hands with her son-in-law, kissed the cheek of her daughter, and climbed into a second-class smoker.

Once the train was in motion, Madame Erling von Bartmann slowly drew her gloves through her hand, from fingers to cuff, stretching them firmly across her knee.

"Ah, how unnecessary."

A BOY ASKS A QUESTION

The days had been very warm and close. It was fall now and everything was drawing in for winter. It had been a bad but somehow pleasant year. It seemed that a great number of people had been disillusioned about one thing or another, or perhaps it was the drought; whatever it was, fewer people were seen hurrying from one place to another; winter with frost and snow would be welcome.

Carmen la Tosca (with a name like that, what could she be but an actress?) was in the habit of riding at a swift gallop down the lane and into the copse beyond. She leaned in the saddle as she went under the boughs, the plume of her hat bending smartly back as she rounded the curve.

Her horse was a bolt of white, with shining fetlock, hard tense descending plane of frontal bone, blowing nostrils; but when Carmen la Tosca broke the line of the horse's back with her own, the spine flowed deftly under her like quick water, quivering into massive haunches, socketing a foaming flair of tail.

She rode well. She dropped her pelvis lightly upon the saddle, she kept her grip purposely slack.

She had been in stock for some time. Earlier on she had been in opera; she had been the queen in *Aida* (among other parts) and she had played boys in vaudeville.

She was not the kind of woman who makes a habit of visiting the country, at least not the sort of country that people refer to as "a jolly place, snuggling among the foothills" . . . not at all, but this particular summer did find her trying out its simple pleasures.

To country folk she was absolutely stupendous. The boys who lolled about the general store said she was "staggering;" smaller children backed away from her when she walked in the road, calling, "Red mouth! Red mouth!"—but no one knew her.

She had appeared in the spring of the year with a man-servant and a maid. She had taken the "chalet," as the long empty house was called. It had two verandahs running clear around, and it had dozens of windows. All three of the new tenants were seen, all at one time, hanging new curtains. When they were in place, no one saw anyone for days, that is, no one saw *her* for days. Then she brought out the white horse and rode it. Before the season was over, she had hired five or six others, but she herself always singled out the white for her own mount. For a while she rode alone, then parties of four or five were seen with her, and now and again a gentleman (a birthmark twisting his face into unwilling scorn) rode beside her. There was a goat-path in the underbrush, here two boys sometimes came, and lying on their stomachs whispered together, waiting for her, walking or riding. The boys were Brandt and Baily Wilson, farmer's sons. Sometimes, having waited in vain, they took the mountain road, berry-buckets in hand, because the mountain road went right past her house, where they could hear her people laughing behind the casement.

Sometimes she walked out, descending the hill, carefully, avoiding the crabgrass and the melon patches, talking brightly to the scarred gentleman, but paying little attention to the effect of her words, not through discourtesy but because she let things drift away.

Of course there was no end to the gossip, she did not court attention, she got attention. People said she was not exactly handsome, but neither was she ugly; her face held a perfect balance of the two—and then she was outrageously "*chic*."

One of the women of the village, who had once, years ago, been to London "to see the Queen," said la Tosca's back was "just like;" this was without doubt sheer nonsense, but it did no harm; indeed, it pleased everyone.

Carmen la Tosca breakfasted in bed, and late. Having caught herself out of sleep in a net of bobbin-lace, she broke fast with both food and scent, lazily dusting her neck and arms with perfumed talc, lolling on the bed (which stood between two ovals of pear-wood, framing versions of Leda and the swan), ripping through the wrappers of Puerto Rican journals and French gazettes with the blade of a murderous paper-cutter, and finally, in the total vacancy of complete indulgence, her hand sprawling across a screaming headline, would stare out into the harsh economy of russet boughs, pranked out in fruit.

The room and its occupant were a total discord. The beams, in that part of the country usually stained with walnut juice, were here jackass grey and plainly pegged, the walls ashen, and the doors, opening into the orchard, let pass a line of ragged grass. Carmen la Tosca liked that; but as the mornings were growing chill, she drew a quilted throw about her, and at night, when it rained, the shutters were thrown open that she might watch it falling down.

The particular morning the boy chose for his daring visit was waist-deep in fog, rain dripped from every branch and leaf, but by eleven the sun had managed to get out. He waited outside the doors until she turned her face to the wall, then he stepped in.

It was Brandt Wilson, fourteen. He was short, his hands, feet and head were large. He was splashed with mud and rumpled. His tie stuck out ridiculously over the top of his tight little vest. He stood before her on the rug, hat in hand.

With a single movement she turned in bed.

"*Well*, who are you?"

"I'm Brandt Wilson, I live out there."

She said without smiling: "What is it?"

The boy hesitated, "I have a brother—"

Carmen la Tosca pushed the papers away, regarding him with amusement.

"Have you?"

"He's older than I am—and you know everything . . ."

"I do, do I. Who said so?"

"Everybody. The postman says you are a 'woman of the world—'"

"Gracious!"

"My brother Baily"—his breaking voice came up in a quivering treble—"well, my sister says, 'I don't like Baily any more—he has lost his plain look.' And I said, 'he's just the same, when you give him a present, and he is bending down untying it.'"

"What is this all about?"

"Out there, on the hill, we were lying in the sun—" he stared at her blankly, "He said he cried when it was over."

"When *what* was over?"

"I don't know; he said, 'I am a man now,' and he grabbed me, and he was crying, and we rolled down the hill. Will I be like that?"

She rose on her elbow and looked at him with suffused eyes.

"How many of you are there?"

"Four."

"And how old is the oldest?"

"Twenty-three. He cried too, about his girl, she died. When they told him, he beat the open door on both sides, and shouted: 'I could have stopped her.' He wouldn't tell us how, but he told mother. 'I would have said I love you.' Is that a power?"

"Yes, it is innocence. We are all waiting for someone who will learn our innocence—all over again." She lay back on her pillow.

"Am *I* going to cry?"

"I don't know, why not? Everyone suffers—all of us. In spite of all the things people say and explain, it is the same thing for everyone; men cry too—men *can* hurt."

He moved his hand on the footboard of the bed.

"I'm sorry," she said, "it's my indolence that does it."

"Does what?"

"Embarrasses you."

"It's all right."

"It is not," she answered. "Do you observe animals?"

He did not answer.

"*Do* you?"

"Yes."

She clapped her hands. "What would all your troubles mean to an animal?"

"I don't know."

"You don't?"

He looked down. "What does it mean?" As he spoke, he forgot what he had come for. "What is going to happen?—"

"Let the evil of the day—"

He said breathlessly. "That's what I want to know—"

"Listen. Do you know what makes the difference between the wise man and the fool? Never do evil to good people, they always forgive, and that's too much for anybody. In the end," she said, "when it is all over, you'll listen to nothing at all; only the simple story, told by everything."

"But I want to know now."

"Now," she said, "now is the time when you leave everything alone."

"But *why* did he cry?"

"Dignity—and despair—and innocence."

"Is that all?"

She had taken up her paper. "That is everything. In the end it will be the death of you."

He did not move.

"Come here," she said, and he came quickly. She drew his head toward her until their foreheads met.

"Start all over again," she said. He went away then.

And that very afternoon, Carmen la Tosca rode off, with her entire *entourage*.

THE PERFECT MURDER

Professor Anatol Profax was nevertheless deeply interested in dialectology. The effect of environment on the tongue had been his life work; he had even gone so far as to assert that the shape of the tongue made people move up or downtown; if it were heavy, large and flat it usually took them to the country, if it were a light tripping member they generally found themselves in Paris. The professor thought that the cutting out of tongues might produce mystics. He was sorry he had no power to try the experiment.

By the time he had reached middle age Professor Profax had pretty well covered his field—no pains had been spared. He had tracked down figures of speech and preferred exclamations in all walks of life; he had conversed with the trained and untrained mind; the loquacious and the inarticulate had been tabulated. The inarticulate had proved particularly satisfactory; they were rather more racial than individual. In England they said "Right!" in Germany they said "Wrong," in France they said "Cow!" in America they said "So what?" These were bunch-indexed or clubbed under *The Inveterates*—it was his sister (now swatting out a thesis on the development of the mandible under vituperation) that got him down. She was always saying: "My God, *can you believe it*!" He classed her as the *Excitable Spinster* type and let it go at that. On the other hand, the scores he had chalked up on defective minors and senile neurotics had proved disappointing. The professor was not even slightly interested in the human whine of the permanently hooked; conversely, he thoroughly enjoyed the healthy alkahest of applied appelatives—they were responsible for the most delightful boggles. What he had yet to lay his hands on was someone who *defied classification*.

Crossing Third Avenue toward Fourteenth Street, Professor Profax pondered the keywords of fanatics, men like Swedenborg and his New Church, Blake and his Bush of Angels. He decided that these gentlemen were quite safe (he had underscored their writings); they had saved themselves by the simple expedient of Getting Out Of Reach.

He thought of his father, a hearty con-conformist who had achieved a quiet insecurity over the dead bodies of John Wesley and early Mormons; who had kicked out the family foot organ in favor of a turning lathe, and who was given to shouting (rather too loudly) "Terrain tumult—ha!"

Deep in the pride of these reflections the professor smiled. He little cared that his figure was followed by many a curious eye. He was indeed old-fashioned. His frock coat was voluminous. Like all creatures that hunt too long he looked hungry. His whole head, which was of polished bone, bore a fine sharp nose, a lightly scored mouth and deep cavernous sockets. He carried a cane over a crooked elbow that tipped inward to hold a worn copy of his book *The Variations*; it was precious in itself, additionally so for the notes on its back pages, made during a trip through the Allegheny Mountains and the fastnesses of Tennessee. He had gone to check up on reactions to the World War. The hill folk had resented the intrusion with dippers smelling strongly of liquor; of the war itself they had only heard as far as prohibition. There was little labial communication. These went under the head *The Impulsive*.

He raised his eyes. A poster depicting the one True and Only Elephant Woman confronted him in bright green and red. He lowered his eyes thinking of Jane Austen; a good tart girl of a *sec* vintage propelled by decency springing to the lash of matrimony. Love—now there was an emotion that had a repetitive vocabulary if ever there was one. It consisted of "Do you love me? Do you *still* love me? You *used* to love me!" Usually this was answered with "Yeah, I love you. Uh huh, I still love you. *What?*" Out west it changed slightly, the interrogative was almost unanimously responded to by "Hell, no!" But one needn't go West. Take his own case, he had never married, yet he was a man of violent passions, wasn't he? He thought this over slowly. Certainly, at some time in his life he must have curbed an emotion, crushed a desire, trampled a weakness. The kerchief in his coat tail fluttered, filled with the dying life of a September noon. Perhaps he was a man who was living on embers and an annuity; a man of worthy memoranda and no parts. Well, it could not be helped now, after all, his Mistress was *Sound*, that great band of sound that had escaped the human throat for over two thousand years. Could it be re-captured (as Marconi thought it might) what would come to the ear? No theories for or against; no words of praise or of blame, only a vast, terrible lamentation which would echo like the "Baum!" of the Malabar Caves. For after all what does man say when it comes right down to it? "I love, I fear, I hunger, I die." Like the cycles of Purgatory and Damnation.

Some years back the professor had thought of doing something about it. He had even tried, but it had been a bit of a failure for, as he recalled sadly, he had been one jigger too elated, had had a swizzle too much (a thing, he was not given to as a rule). This Holy Grail of the Past has eluded him, fool that he was, and had become only a dull longing which he had satisfied by calling in the local firemen and the Salvation Army. He had offered them libations of Montenegrin rum (which he kept hid in the darkness of his Canterbury) . . . ; he had even tried to explain himself; somehow, he had got nowhere. The firemen had not made him happy; the little woman in the Booth bonnet had not saved him. He remembered that he had pressed a five-dollar bill into the hand of the one to remove the other. It had all been a most frightful fluke. He had ended weeping in his den, pen in hand, trying to write a legible note on his blotter to President Wilson; the trend was to the effect that he considered *kumiss* preferable to bottled beer. He had to read it in the mirror the next morning, his head tied up in a towel. Somehow, he had written it back-hand and upside down. In general, he tried to think that he had had a religious experience, but he said nothing about it.

At this moment someone in flowing black bowled into him. He reeled a step, recovered his balance, recrooked his cane and took off his hat.

"Heavenly!" she said. She carried a muff; the strap of one of her satin shoes was loose, her long yellow hair swung back as she caught up her velvet train. "Heavenly!" she breathed.

"What?" said the professor, "I beg your pardon."

"Dying!" she said taking his arm. "I am shallow until you get used to me. If it were not so early, I'd suggest tripes and a pint of bitters."

"Britain," he muttered, "that stern, that great country. How did *you* get here?"

"But it *is* too early."

"Are you the elephant girl?"

"Sometimes, sometimes I work on the trapeze, sometimes I'm a milliner, sometimes I'm hungry." She was thinking. "I'm so fond of the austerities—you know, Plato and all that. He said, 'Seek the truth, and take the longest way,' didn't he?"

"I don't know."

"I just died," she said, "but I came back, I always do. I hate being safe, so I let the bar go and I flew out, right out into you as a matter of fact—"

They had come to the park, and now she released his arm, leaning against the rim of the fountain bowl. "I'm devoted to coming back, it's so agonizing." She swung her foot in its loose shoe, looking at him with her bright honest eyes. "I'm an awful fool when I'm uncomfortable."

"Are you uncomfortable?" he inquired, facing her all in black. "I shall be." she paused, "You see, what is really wrong is that I'm not properly believed; people are wicked because they do not know that I am a *Trauma*."

"I know."

"Do you! That's wonderful. Nobody trusts me. Only last night that beast of a sword swallower (yesterday was Sunday you remember) refused to swallow six of my kitchen knives, he said it would spoil him for the canticles!" She threw her arm out (a velvet band with a bright red rosette was on its wrist). "Imagine! Such perfidy, such incredible cowardice!" she sighed. "Man is a worm and won't risk discredit, and discredit is the *only* beauty. People don't believe me because they don't like my discredits. For instance, I love danger, yet if anyone put a hand on me, I'd yell like murder. Perhaps you heard me yell a moment ago, perhaps you even thought, 'The girl is afraid.' How stupid you are."

"Wait a minute," said the professor, "*Did* you yell?"

Two large tears rolled down her cheeks. "Do *you* doubt me? You bet I yelled."

"Lob." muttered Professor Profax, "Toss, bowl or send forth with a slow or high-pitched underhand motion—lob."

"Wrong." She steered him back across the street, pressing her face against a confectioner's window. "I'm vindictive because I have a *passionate* inferiority; most people have a *submissive* inferiority. It makes all the difference in the world. I am as aboveboard as the Devil. I'd like some caramels."

He bought her a bag of caramels. He was a queer lead color.

"For instance, I'm lovable and offensive. *Imagine that position!*"

"Do you play dominos?"

"No. I want to be married." She blinked her eyes, she was crying again. "You see how it is, it is always too late. I have never been married and yet I am a widow. Think of feeling like that! Oh!" she said, "it's the things I can't stand that drew people to me. It has made me muscular. If I could be hacked down without sentiment I'd be saved. It's the false pride in violence that I abominate. *Why should he be there?*"

"Who?" said the professor nervously.

"The villain." She was smiling.

The professor was beginning to feel that a great work (which he thought he had written) was now hardly readable. He thought grimly, "Poor child, I'd like to support her." He drew himself up with a jerk. "I'd like to have her on my hands, it's the only way I can get rid of her."

"Yes," she said, "we might as well get married—time will pass."

"How about coffee?" he suggested. She nodded. "Tired and vigorous," he said to himself, "What a girl."

She turned him toward Third Avenue. How the dickens did she know it was East not West that his rooms lay.

"Shall we get married today or later?"

"Later," the professor said. "Later will do." He walked slightly listing, she was hanging on his arm, she had forgotten the train of her velvet dress, it was sweeping through the dust, dragging cigarette butts and the stubs of theatre tickets.

"I love enemies," she said, "and Mozart." She turned her head from side to side looking about her nearsightedly. "Let's never make a malleable mistake, do you mind!" She was taller than he, it was odd. "I can't stand my friends," she said, "except for hours."

"Extraordinary," he muttered, "I don't know how to class you."

She drew back with a cry. "Class me! My god, people *love* me!"

She was a little blind in the darkness of the staircase. "People ADORE me—after a long time, after I have told them how beastly they are—weak and sinful—most cases are like that, lovely people. All my friends are common and priceless."

He opened the door and she entered by a series of backward leans, turning shoulder blade after shoulder into the room. He took her muff and laid it down among his guitars and dictionaries—why on earth a muff in September? She did not sit down, at the same time she did not look at anything. She said: "You can criticize people as much as you like if you tell them they are wonderful. Ever try it?"

"No."

"Try it." She pulled her dress about her feet. "I want you to understand, from the beginning, that I am the purest abomination imaginable." She sat down on the trunk. "And my father says that I am so innocent and hard-pressed he's always expecting me to fall out of a book."

He fumbled with his hat, cane, notes. They all fell to the floor.

She sat like a schoolgirl, her knees drawn up, her head bent.

"You're a sedentary. *I* take solitude standing up. I'm a little knock-kneed," she added honestly, "and I want to be good."

Professor Profax put the kettle on. "Would you mind," he said, his back to her, "falling in with yourself until I light the fire."

A stifled scream turned him. She had fallen face down among a pile of musical instruments, knocking over the Canterbury, sending sheet music fluttering into the air. She was pounding her fist among the scattered caramels. Her fist was full of them.

At that precise moment Professor Anatol Profax experienced something he had never experienced before. He felt cold, dedicated and gentle. His heart beat with a thin happy movement. He leaned over. With one firm precise gesture he drew his penknife across her throat.

He lifted the heavy leather lid of the trunk and put her in, piece by piece, the velvet of her gown held her. He laid the toppled head on top of the lace at the neck. She looked like the Scape-Goat, the Paschal Lamb. Suddenly the professor's strength went out of him: he lay down on the floor beside her. He did not know what to do; he had destroyed definition; by his own act he had ruined a great secret; he'd never be able to place her. He shook all over, and still shaking he rose to his knees, his hands out before him, the heel of each he placed on the corners of the lid and raised it.

She was not there.

He clattered out into the street waving for a cab. He did not notice that the vehicle answering his call was one of those hansoms now found nowhere except at the Plaza. He climbed in slamming the little door. "Anywhere!" he shouted to the driver and slumped into the corner. The horse started at the crack of the whip, jogging the leaning face of the professor which was pressed against the glass.

Then he saw the cab's twin. Breast to breast they moved out into the traffic. *She* was in the other. She too was leaning her face against the glass of the window, only her face was pressed against it as she had pressed it against the confectioner's! Her hair fell across her mouth, that great blasphemous mouth which smiled.

The professor tried to move. He tried to call. He was helpless, only his mind went on ticking. "It's the potentialities, not the accomplishment . . . if only I had gotten her name . . . fool! fool? What *was* her name! . . . Lost, lost . . . something extraordinary . . . I've let it slip right through my fingers . . ."

Behind the mists of the two sheets of glass they rode facing each other. A van came in between them. A traffic light separated them.

CASSATION

"Do you know Germany, Madame, Germany in the spring? It is charming then, do you not think so? Wide and clean, the Spree winding thin and dark—and the roses! the yellow roses in the windows; and the bright talkative Americans passing through groups of German men staring over their steins, at the light and laughing women.

"It was such a spring, three years ago, that I came into Berlin from Russia. I was just sixteen, and my heart was a dancer's heart. It is that way sometimes; one's heart is all one thing for months, then—altogether another thing, *nicht wahr?* I used to sit in the café at the end of the Zelten, eating eggs and drinking coffee, watching the sudden rain of sparrows. Their feet struck the table all together, and all together they cleared the crumbs, and all together they flew into the sky, so that the café was as suddenly without birds as it had been suddenly full of birds.

"Sometimes a woman came here, at about the same hour as myself, around four in the afternoon; once she came with a little man, quite dreamy and uncertain. But I must explain how she looked: *temperamentvoll* and tall, *kraftvoll* and thin. She must have been forty then, dressed richly and carelessly. It seemed as though she could hardly keep her clothes on; her shoulders were always coming out, her skirt would be hanging on a hook, her pocketbook would be mislaid, but all the time she was savage with jewels, and something purposeful and dramatic came in with her, as if she were the center of a whirlpool, and her clothes a temporary debris.

"Sometimes she clucked the sparrows, and sometimes she talked to the *Weinschenk*. Clasping her fingers together until the rings stood out and you could see through them, she was so vital and so wasted. As for her dainty little man, she would talk to him in English, so that I did not know where they came from.

"Then one week I stayed away from the café because I was trying out for the *Schauspielhaus*, I heard they wanted a ballet dancer, and I was very anxious to get the part, so of course I thought of nothing else. I would wander, all by myself, through the *Tiergarten*, or I would stroll down the *Sieges-Allee* where all the great German emperors' statues are, looking like widows. Then suddenly I thought of the Zelten, and of the birds, and of that tall, odd woman and so I went back there, and there she was, sitting in the garden sipping beer and chuck-chucking the sparrows.

"When I came in, she got up at once and came over to me and said: 'Why, how do you do, I have missed you. Why did you not tell me that you were going away? I should have seen what I could do about it.'

"She talked like that; a voice that touched the heart because it was so unbroken and clear. 'I have a house,' she said, 'just on the Spree. You could have stayed with me. It is a big, large house, and you could have the room just off my room. It is difficult to live in, but it is lovely—Italian you know, like the interiors you see in Venetian paintings, where young girls lie dreaming of the Virgin. You could find that you could sleep there, because you have dedication.'

"Somehow it did not seem at all out of the way that she should come to me and speak to me. I said I would meet her again some day in the garden, and we could go 'home' together, and she seemed pleased, but did not show surprise.

"Then one evening we came into the garden at the same moment. It was late and the fiddles were already playing. We sat together without speaking, just listening to the music, and admiring the playing of the only woman member of the orchestra. She was very intent on the movement of her fingers and seemed to be leaning over her chin to watch. Then suddenly the lady got up, leaving a small rain of coin, and I followed her until we came to a big house, and she let herself in with a brass key. She turned to the left and went into a dark room and switched on the lights and sat down and said: 'This is where we sleep; this is how it is.'

"Everything was disorderly, and expensive and melancholy. Everything was massive and tall, or broad and wide. A chest of drawers rose above my head. The china stove was enormous and white, enameled in blue flowers. The bed was so high that you could only think of it as something that might be overcome. The walls were all bookshelves, and all the books were bound in red morocco, on the back of each, in gold, was stamped a coat of arms, intricate and oppressive. She rang for tea and began taking off her hat.

"A great painting hung over the bed; the painting and the bed ran together in encounter, the huge rumps of the stallions reined into the pillows. The generals, with foreign helmets and dripping swords, raging through rolling smoke and the bleeding ranks of the dying, seemed to be charging the bed, so large, so rumpled, so devastated. The sheets were trailing, the counterpane hung torn, and the feathers shivered along the floor, trembling in the slight wind from the open window. The lady was smiling in a sad grave way, but she said nothing, and it was not until some moments later that I saw a child, not more than three years old, a small child, lying in the center of the pillows, making a thin noise, like the buzzing of a fly, and I thought it was a fly.

"She did not talk to the child, indeed she paid no attention to it, as if it were in her bed and she did not know it. When the tea was brought in, she poured it, but she took none, instead she drank small glasses of Rhine wine.

"'You have seen Ludwig,' she said in her faint and grieving voice, 'we were married a long time ago, he was just a boy then. I? Me? I am an Italian, but I studied English and German because I was with a travelling company. You,' she said abruptly, 'you must give up the ballet—the theater—acting.' Somehow, I did not think it odd that she should know of my ambition, though I had not mentioned it. 'And,' she went on, 'you are not for the stage; you are for something quieter, more withdrawn. See here, I like Germany very much, I have lived here a good many years. You will stay and you will see. You have seen Ludwig, you have noticed that he is not strong; he is always de-clining, you must have noticed it yourself; he must not be distressed, he can't bear anything. He has his room to himself.' She seemed suddenly tired, and she got up and threw herself across the bed, at the foot, and fell asleep, almost instantly, her hair all about her. I went away then, but I came back that night and tapped at the window. She came to the window and signed to me, and presently appeared at another window to the right of the bedroom, and beckoned with her hand, and I came up and climbed in, and did not mind that she had not opened the door for me. The room was dark except for the moon, and two thin candles burning before the Virgin.

"It was a beautiful room, Madame, '*traurig*' as she said. Everything was important and old and gloomy. The cur-tains about the bed were red velvet, Italian you know, and fringed in gold bullion. The bed cover was a deep red velvet with the same gold fringe: on the floor, beside the bed, a stand on which was a tasseled red cushion, on the cushion a Bible in Italian, lying open.

"She gave me a long nightgown, it came below my feet and came back up again almost to my knees. She loosened my hair, it was long then, and yellow. She plaited it in two plaits; she put me down at her side and said a prayer in German, then in Italian, and ended, 'God bless you,' and I got into bed. I loved her very much because there was nothing between us but this strange preparation for sleep. She went away then. In the night I heard the child crying, but I was tired.

"I stayed a year. The thought of the stage had gone out of my heart. I had become a *religieuse*; a gentle religion that began with the prayer I had said after her the first night, and the way I had gone to sleep, though we never repeated the ceremony. It grew with the furniture and the air of the whole room, and with the Bible lying open at a page that I could not read; a religion, Madame, that was empty of need, therefore it was not holy perhaps, and not as it should have been in its manner. It was that I was happy, and I lived there for one year. I almost never saw Ludwig, and almost never Valentine, for that was her child's name, a little girl.

"But at the end of that year I knew there was trouble in other parts of the house. I heard her walking in the night, sometimes Ludwig would be with her, I could hear him crying and talking, but I could not hear what was said. It sounded like a sort of lesson, a lesson for a child to repeat, but if so, there would have been no answer, for the child never uttered a sound, except that buzzing cry.

"Sometimes it is wonderful in Germany, Madame, *nicht wahr*? There is nothing like a German winter. She and I used to walk about the Imperial Palace, and she stroked the cannon, and said they were splendid. We talked about philosophy, for she was troubled with too much thinking, but she always came to the same conclusion, that one must be, or try to be, like everyone else. She explained that to be like everyone, all at once, in your own person, was to be holy. She said that people did not understand what was meant by 'Love thy neighbor as thyself.' It meant, she said, that one should be like all people and oneself, then, she said, one was both ruined and powerful.

"Sometimes it seemed that she was managing it, that she was all Germany, at least in her Italian heart. She seemed so irreparably collected and yet distressed, that I was afraid of her, and not afraid.

"That is the way it was, Madame, she seemed to wish it to be that way, though at night she was most scattered and distraught, I could hear her pacing in her room.

"Then she came in one night and woke me and said that I must come into her room. It was in a most terrible disorder. There was a small cot bed that had not been there before. She pointed to it and said that it was for me.

"The child was lying in the great bed against a large lace pillow. Now it was four years old and yet it did not walk, and I never heard it say a thing, or make a sound, except that buzzing cry. It was beautiful in the corrupt way of idiot children; a sacred beast without a taker, tainted with innocence and waste time; honey-haired and failing, like those dwarf angels on holy prints and valentines, if you understand me, Madame, something saved for a special day that would not arrive, not for life at all: and my lady was talking quietly, but I did not recognize any of her former state.

"'You must sleep here now,' she said, 'I brought you here for this if I should need you, and I need you. You must stay, you must stay forever.' Then she said, 'Will you?' And I said no, I could not do that.

"She took up the candle and put it on the floor beside me, and knelt beside it, and put her arms about my knees. 'Are you a traitor?' she said, 'have you come into my house, Ludwig's house, the house of my child, to betray us?' And I said, no, I had not come to betray. 'Then,' she said, 'you will do as I tell you. I will teach you slowly, slowly; it will not be too much for you, but you must begin to forget, you must forget everything. You must forget all the things people have told you. You must forget arguments and philosophy. I was wrong in talking of such things; I thought it would teach you how to lag with her mind, to undo time for her as it passes, to climb into her bereavement and her dispossession. I brought you up badly; I was vain. You will do better. Forgive me.' She put the palms of her hands on the floor, her face to my face. 'You must never see any other room than this room. It was a great vanity that I took you out walking. Now you will stay here safely, and you will see. You will like it, you will learn to like it the very best of all. I will bring you breakfast, and luncheon, and supper. I will bring it to you both, myself. I will hold you on my lap, I will feed you like the birds. I will rock you to sleep. You must not argue with me—above all we must have no arguments, no talk about man and his destiny—man has no destiny—that is my secret—I have been keeping it from you until today, this very hour. Why not before? Perhaps I was jealous of the knowledge, yes, that must be it, but now I give it to you, I share it with you. I am an old woman,' she said, still holding me by the knees. 'When Valentine was born, Ludwig was only a boy.' She got up and stood behind me. 'He is not strong, he does not understand that the weak are the strongest things in the world, because he is one of them. He cannot help her, they are adamant together. I need you, it must be you.' Suddenly she began talking to me as she talked with the child, and I did not know which of us she was talking to. 'Do not repeat anything after me. Why should children repeat what people say? The whole world is nothing but a noise, as hot as the inside of a tiger's mouth. They call it civilization—that is a lie! But some day you may have to go out, someone will try to take you out, and you will not understand them or what they are saying, unless you understand nothing, absolutely nothing, then you will manage.' She moved around so that she faced us, her back against the wall. 'Look,' she said, 'it is all over, it has gone away, you do not need to be afraid; there is only you. The stars are out, and the snow is falling down and covering the world, the hedges, the houses and the lamps. No, no!' she said to herself, 'wait. I will put you on your feet, and tie you up in ribbons, and we will go out together, out into the garden where the swans are, and the flowers and the bees and small beasts. And the students will come, because it will be summer, and they will read in their books . . .' She broke off, then took her wild speech up again, this time as though she were really speaking to the child, 'Katya will go with you. She will instruct you, she will tell you there are no swans, no flowers, no beasts, no boys—nothing, nothing at all, just as you like it. No mind, no thought, nothing whatsoever else. No bells will ring, no people will talk, no birds will fly, no boys will move, there'll be no birth and no death; no sorrow, no laughing, no kissing, no crying, no terror, no joy; no eating, no drinking, no games, no dancing; no father, no mother, no sisters, no brothers—only you, only you!'

"I stopped her, and I said, 'Gaya, why is it that you suffer so, and what am I to do?' I tried to put my arms around her, but she struck them down crying, 'Silence!' Then she said, bringing her face close to my face, 'She has no claws to hang by; she has no hunting foot; she has no mouth for the meat—vacancy!'

"Then, Madame, I got up. It was very cold in the room. I went to the window and pulled the curtain, it was a bright and starry night, and I stood leaning my head against the frame, saying nothing. When I turned around, she was regarding me, her hands held apart, and I knew that I had to go away and leave her. So I came up to her and said, 'Good-bye, my Lady.' And I went and put on my street clothes, and when I came back, she was leaning against the battle picture, her hands hanging. I said to her, without approaching her, 'Good-bye, my love,' and went away.

"Sometimes it is beautiful in Berlin, Madame, *nicht wahr*? There was something new in my heart, a passion to see Paris, so it was natural that I said *lebe wohl* to Berlin.

"I went for the last time to the café in the Zelten, ate my eggs, drank my coffee and watched the birds coming and going just as they used to come and go—altogether here then altogether gone. I was happy in my spirit, for that is the way it is with my spirit, Madame, when I am going away.

"But I went back to her house just once. I went in quite easily by the door, for all the doors and windows were open—perhaps they were sweeping that day. I came to the bedroom door and knocked, but there was no answer. I pushed, and there she was, sitting up in the bed with the child, and she and the child were making that buzzing cry, and no human sound between them, and as usual, everything was in disorder. I came up to her, but she did not seem to know me. I said, 'I am going away; I am going to Paris. There is a longing in me to be in Paris. So I have come to say farewell.'

"She got down off the bed and came to the door with me. She said, 'Forgive me—I trusted you—I was mistaken. I did not know that I could do it myself, but you see, I can do it myself.' Then she got back on to the bed and said, 'Go away,' and I went.

"Things are like that, when one travels, *nicht wahr*, Madame?"

THE GRANDE MALADE

"And there we were, my sister Moydia and I, Madame. Moydia was fifteen and I was seventeen and we were young all over. Moydia has a thin skin, so that I sit and look at her and wonder how she has opinions. She is all white except the cheekbones, then rosy red; her teeth are milk-teeth, and she has a small figure, very pretty and droll. She wanted to become '*tragique*' and '*triste*' and 'tremendous' all at once, like the great period Frenchwomen, only fiercer and perhaps less pure, and yet to die and give up the heart like a virgin. It was a noble, an impossible ambition, *n'est-ce pas*, Madame? But that was the way it was with Moydia. We used to sit in the sun when we were in Norway and read Goethe and did not agree with him at all. 'The man is *pompeux* and too *assuré*,' she would say, shutting her teeth, 'and very much too *facile*.' But then, people say we do not know.

"We are Russian, Moydia and I, and but for an accident, the most terrifying of our life up to then, we would not have known that our grandmother was a Jew—why? because she was *allowed* to drink champagne on her deathbed, and Jews are forbidden champagne you know. So, being 'damned' as it were (both in her dying *and* the 'permission,') she forced mother to drink champagne too, that she might be damned in living as the dying in extremity. So we are Jew and not Jew. We are where we are. We are Polish when we are in Poland, and when in Holland we are Dutch, and now in France we are French, and one day we will go to America and be American; you will see, Madame.

"Now I have forgotten all the Polish I knew and all the Russian I knew and all the Dutch, except, that is, a poem. Ah, that poem, that small piece of a poem! a very touching thing, heavy, sweet—a fragment of language. It makes you feel pity in your whole body, because it is complete but mutilated, like a Greek statue, yet whole, like a life, Madame.

"Now I have come to Paris, and I respect Paris. First, I respected it in a great hat. I am short and a great hat would not, you see, become me, but I wore it for respect. It was all a jumble of flowers and one limber feather; it stood out so that my face was in the middle of a garden. Now I do not wear it any more. I have had to go back in my knowledge, right back to the remembrance, which is the place where I regard my father, and how he looked when in from the new snow. I did not really see him then. Now I see he was truly beautiful all the time that I was thinking nothing about him at all—his astrakhan cap, his frogged coat, with all those silver buttons, and the tall shining boots that caught him just under the knee. Then I think of the window I looked down from and saw the crown of that hat—a wonderful, a mysterious red felt. So now, out of respect for that man, I wear my hats small. Some day, when I have money, my shoes will be higher and come under my knee. This is my way, Madame, but it is not the way it is with Moydia. She has a *great memory in the present*, and it all turns about a cape, therefore now she wears a cape, until something yet more austere drives the cape away. But I must explain.

"First, we are very young as I said, so because of that one becomes *tragique* very quickly, if one is brave, is it not so? So Moydia, though she is two years younger than I, became exhausted almost at once.

"You know how it is in Paris in the autumn, when the summer is just giving up the leaf. I had been here with Moydia two autumns; the first was sad and light on the heart, the way it is when all one's lovers live in spite of the cold. We walked in the Tuileries, I in my small cap and Moydia in a woolly coat, for that was the kind of coat she wore then, and we bought pink and blue candies outside the Punch and Judy show and laughed when the puppets beat each other, Moydia's face tight beneath her skin with the lemon flavor, and tears coming down from her eyes as we thought how perfect everything was; the dolls at their fight and the trees bare, the ground all shuffled in with their foliage—then the pond. We stopped at the pond. The water was full to the edge with water-lily pads and Moydia said it was a shame that women threw themselves in the Seine, only to become a part of its sorrow, instead of casting themselves into a just-right pond like this, where the water would become a part of them. We felt a great despair that people do not live or die beautifully, nor plan anything at all; and then and there we said we would do better.

"After that I noticed, almost at once, that Moydia had become a little too florid. She sprinkled her sugar in her tea from too great a height, and she talked very fast. That was how it was with my sister Moydia in that autumn.

"And of course sophistication came upon us suddenly. We hung long curtains over our beds, and we talked of lovers, and we smoked. And me? I went about in satin trousers for respect to China, which is a very great country and has *majesté* because you cannot know it. It is like a big book which you can read but not understand. So I talked of China to Moydia; and we kept three birds that did not sing, as a symbol of the Chinese heart; and Moydia lay on her bed and became more and more restless, like a story that has no beginning and no end, only a passion like flash lightning.

"She was always kicking her feet in the air and tearing handkerchiefs and crying in her pillow, but when I asked her why she was doing all this, she sat straight up, wailing, 'Because I want *everything*, and to be consumed in my youth!'

"So one day she knew everything. Though I am two years older than Moydia, it is different with me. I live more slowly, only women listen to me, but men adore Moydia. To her they do not listen, they look. They look at her when she sits down and when she walks. All at once she began to walk and to sit down quite differently. All her movements were a sort of *malheureuse* tempest. She had her lover and she laughed and cried, lying face down, and whimpering, 'Isn't it *wonderful*!' And perhaps it was indeed wonderful, Madame. From all her admirers she had chosen the most famous, none other than Monsieur X. His great notoriety had thinned him. He dressed very *soigneusement*; white gloves, you know, and spats and a cape, a very handsome affair with a military collar; and he was *grave* and *rare* and stared at you with one eye not at all, but the other looked out from a monocle, like the lidless eye of a fish that keeps deep water. He was the *protégé* of a Baron. The Baron liked him very much and called him his '*Poupon prodigieux*,' and they played farces together for the amusement of the Faubourg. That was the way it was with Monsieur X, at least in his season when he was, shall we say, the *belle-d'un-jour* and was occupied in writing fables on mice and men, but he always ended the stories with paragraphs *très acre* against women.

"Moydia began to cultivate a throaty voice. She became an *habitué* of the opera; fierce and fluttering, she danced about Monsieur X during the *entr'acte*, pulling her flowers to pieces and scattering them as she went, humming, '*Je suis éternellement!*' The audience looked on with displeasure, but the Baron was enchanted.

"Because I and my sister have always been much together, we were much together now. Sometimes I visited the Baron with her and had many hours of dignity just watching them. When the Baron was entertaining, he was very gay and had great control of a sort of aged immaturity, and Moydia would play the kitten or the great lady, as the occasion demanded. If he seemed to forget her for an instant, she became a *gamine*, sticking her tongue out at his turned back, hissing, '*Ah, tu es belle!*' at which he would turn about and laugh, she falling into his lap, all in one piece, stiff and *enragé*. And he would have a long time stroking her and asking her, in his light worn feminine voice, what was the matter. And once she would not open her eyes, but screamed and made him hold her heart, saying, 'Does not the creature beat dreadfully?' and he entreated her, 'Because? Because?'

"Then clapping her hands, she would burst into tears and cry: 'I give you too many destinies with my body. I am Marie on the way to the *guillotine*. I am Bloody Mary, but I have not seen blood. I am Desdemona, but Othello—where is he? I am Hecuba and Helen. I am Graetal and Brunhilda, I am Nana and Camille. But I'm not as bored as they are! When shall I become *properly* bored?'

"He was bored, and he put her off his knee. She flew at him then and pulled his clothes about and ripped his gloves and said with absolute quiet: 'It amazes me how I do not love you.'

"But when we got home, I had to put her to bed. She was shivering and laughing, and she seemed to be running a fever.

"'Did you see his face? He is a monster! A product of *malaise*. He *wants* me to be his sacristan. He'd like me to bury him. I am positive of it, Katya; are you not positive of it? He is an old soul. He has come to his mortal end. He is beastly with *finis*. But Death has given him leave. Oh!' she cried, 'I adore him! I adore him! I adore him! Oh, I do adore him!' And she refused to see him until he went quite out of his head and called for himself. She went running before him all down the hall. I could hear the sharp report of her heels, and her lisping voice quoting: '*Le héron au long bec emmanché d'un long cou*,' in a singsong as she jumped the last step into the day, exclaiming, '*C'est la Fontaine, la*

Fontaine magnifique!' And you could hear his cane tapping after her.

"Then this last autumn, before this last winter set in (you were not here then, Madame), Moydia had gone to Germany to visit papa, and all the night before we had sat up together, the three of us, Moydia, her lover and I. We drank a great deal too much, I sang my Dutch song and talked a long time, rambling on about father and his cap and boots, and that splendid coat of his. It pleased Moydia and it pleased me, but to Monsieur X, probably we seemed like beggars recalling remembered gold. So I danced a Tartar dance and raged that my boots did not reach to my knees, and all the time Moydia was lying on her lover's shoulder, both welded as if they were an emblem. But when I stopped whirling, he called me over, and he whispered that I should have a pair of great boots some day, which gave me great joy. But Moydia sprang up. 'I do not love this man, Cookoo, do I?' She always called him Cookoo when she was most fond, as though she were talking about someone else. 'I only love Cookoo when I am drunk. So now I do not love him at all, because I am not drunk at all. Oh, we Russian women drink a great deal, but it is to become sober—this is something the other peoples do not take into account! Is it not so, Katya? It's because we are so extravagant that we do not reach justice . . . we reach poetry. You adore me, you see,' she said to him, 'and I *let* you, but that is the way it is with Polish women.'

"'Russian,' he corrected, and sat staring through the boss of his monocle straight at the wall.

"Well then, Moydia went away to Germany to visit papa, who is a travelling man now and buys and sells diamonds. He will not send us money unless he sees us at least once a year. He's that way. He says he will not have his girls grow up into something he does not like paying for. Sometimes he sends money from Russia, sometimes from Poland, sometimes from Belgium, sometimes from England. He has said that some day he will come to Paris, but he does not come. It is very confusing to get so many kinds of moneys, we never know what we will have to spend, we have to be very careful; perhaps that is the whole idea. But at this point Moydia had lost all caution. She bought herself a new dress to please Monsieur X, and to go away in, and not to alarm father—all at the same time. So it was a cunning dress, very deft and touching. It was all dotted suisse, with a very tight bodice, and into this bodice, just between the breasts, was embroidered, in very fine twist, a slain lamb. It might, you see, mean everything and it might mean nothing, and it might bring pleasure to both father and lover.

"After she had gone, I sat in the café every afternoon and waited for her return. She was not to be gone longer than two weeks. That was the autumn that I felt great sadness, Madame, I read a great deal and I walked about all by myself; I was in need of solitude. I walked in the Tuileries and visited the pond again and went under the trees where the air was cool and there were numbers of people who did not seem to be gay. The autumn had come differently this year; it was already oppressive in September—it was as though there were a catafalque coming into Paris from a long way and everyone knew it; men buttoned their coats tight and the women tipped their sunshades down, as if for rain.

"So ten days passed, and the season hung heavy in a mist that blotted almost everything out. You could scarcely see the Seine when you went walking on the bridges, the statues in the parks were altogether withdrawn, the sentries looked like dolls in boxes, the ground was always damp, the café *brasiers* were going full heat. Then I knew, suddenly I knew—Moydia's lover was dying! And indeed, that night he died. He had caught a chill the evening that Moydia left, and it had grown worse and worse. It was reported the Baron was always with him, and when the Baron saw that Monsieur X was truly going to die, he made him drink. They drank together all night and into the morning. The Baron wanted it that way: 'For that,' he said, 'he might die as he was born, without knowing.'

"So I went straight to the Baron's house, and right up to the door, and rapped—but he would not let me in. He said through the door that Moydia's lover had been buried that very morning, and I said, 'Give me something for Moydia,' and he said, 'What shall I give you?' and he added, 'He left nothing but a deathless name!' And I said, 'Give me his cape.' And he gave me his cape, through the leeway of the chain on the door, but he did not look out at me, and I went away.

"That night Moydia arrived back from Germany. She had a terrible fever and she talked very fast, like a child. She wanted to go directly to Monsieur's house; I had great difficulty in keeping her in. I put her to bed and made her tea, but I could not keep still, so I brought her the cape and I said, 'Cookoo is dead, and this is his cape and it is for you.' She said, 'How did he die?' and 'Why?'

"I said, 'He was taken ill the night you left, and it became a fever that would not leave him, so the Baron sat with him, and they drank all night that he might die as he was born, without knowing.'

"Moydia began beating on the bed then with both hands and saying, 'Let us drink, and pray God I shall die the same death!' We sat up all night drinking and talking together without much sense. Toward morning she said, 'Now I have a great life!' and she wept and went to sleep, and by noon she was quite well.

"Now, Madame, she wears it always. The cape. Men admire her in it, indeed she looks very well in it, do you not think so? She has grown faster than I; you would take her for the elder, would you not? She is gay, spoiled, *tragique*. She sugars her tea from far too great a height. And that's all. There's nothing else to tell, except—in the debacle my boots were quite forgotten. The next day all the papers carried pages and pages about Monsieur X, and in all of them he was wearing a cape. We, Moydia and I, read them together. They may even have printed something about him in America? Truly, we speak a little French; now we must be moving on."

DUSIE

It is about Dusie, Madame, she was very young, perhaps only a year older than I, and tall, very big and beautiful, absent and so pale. She wore big shoes, and her ankles and wrists were large, and her legs beyond belief long. She used to sit in the corner of the café, day after day, drinking, and she had a bitter careless sort of ferocity with women. Not in anything she said, for she spoke seldom, but she handled them roughly, yet gladly. She was *dégagé*, but you could not know her well.

Sometimes, walking down the Rue D—, I saw her standing out on the balcony of her room, in a white dressing gown, like a man's, and sometimes she called to me, if she was not singing, and sometimes she did not. So it is with people in Paris, *n'est-ce-pas?*

After a while I did not see her in the café much, but often in the house of Madame K—. It was a splendid house, with footmen standing behind the great iron doors, in white gloves. They looked always as if they expected you, yet did not care.

The house was very French. All gold and blue, and, in the boudoirs, pink. There were three, but the part of the house I saw most often was blue and white, with much lace and gold. The walls were blue satin, and hanging from tasseled cords were many golden framed women hung. They were all reclining, and they looked at you sideways, smiling from beneath hives of honey-colored hair, and they had little with them but birds and flowers, and all were anemic and charming, as if they had been handled too much. Sometimes a bar of music was near to them, but you would not think of humming it, it so belonged to them, just as it was.

There were many chrysanthemums, and a long white harp in the embrasure of the window, and in the dust lying upon it many women had written "Dusie." And above all, in an enameled cage, two canaries, the one who sang, and the one who listened.

But in the boudoirs, there was much pink, and everything was brittle and glazed and intricate. Ribbons dangled from everything and bon-bons were everywhere, and statuettes of little boys in satin breeches, offering tiny ladies in bouffant skirts, fans and finches and flowers, and all about in the grass were stuck shiny slinking foxes.

A thin powder was over everything upon the dressing table, mauve and sweet smelling, and a great litter of *La Vie Parisienne* and *Le Rire*, and when you picked up the most solemn looking volume, engravings of Watteau fell out and Greuze, and in the hall a tall clock tinkled and rang.

Madame K— was large, very full and blond. She went with the furniture as only a childless Frenchwoman can. She had been a surgeon, a physician, but nothing remained of it, only the tone of her voice when she was angry; then she removed the argument within the exact bounds of its sickness.

When there was talk of spiritual matters, and there is always such talk, Madame, when women, many women, are closed up together in a room, she listened, but she let you know definitely that she was mortal.

There were always a large number of women in her house. It was like a Northern *gare*, and no trains running. There especially was Clarissa.

With Clarissa it was like this: it was as if everyone was her torment, as if she lived only because so many people had seen and spoken to her and of her. If she had been forgotten for a month, entirely, by everyone, I am sure she would have died. Everyone was her wound, and this made her sly, and sweet, and attractive too. For alone of them all, Madame K— had the great indifference for her, and was about her in no way occupied at all.

But for Dusie, Madame K— had love. You knew, because when Dusie was with her, Madame K— looked like a precaution all at once.

For that is the way it was with Dusie always. All people gave her their attention, stroking her, and calling her pet or beast, according to their feelings. They touched her as if she were an idol, and she stood tall, or sat to drink, unheeding, absent. You felt that you must talk to Dusie, tell her everything, because all her beauty was there, but uninhabited, like a church, *n'est-ce-pas*, Madame? Only she was not holy, she was very mortal, and sometimes vulgar, a ferocious and oblivious vulgarity. She cursed when corks would not come out of bottles; when women moved their knees if she were lying on them; when someone said men were wise.

She had long, heavy hair, yet it looked like a splendid shame, and I could not tell why. Then one time, in Mi-Carême, she cut it away; she said she had done it to be just. No one knew quite what she meant.

It is simple to understand why it was good to be near her. She had a strong bodily odor, like sleep and a tree growing, and yet she was not strong. Her movements were like vines growing over a ruin. When she was ill it was sorrowful to see her, she suffered such shallow pain, as if her body were in the toils of a feeble and remorseless agony. Then she would lie over, her knees up, her head down, laughing and crying and saying, "Do you love me?" to every woman, and every woman answered that they loved her. But it did not change her, and suddenly she would shout: "Get out, get out of my room!" Something in her grew and died for her alone.

When they were gone, thrown out, she would sit up in bed and amuse herself with the dolls they had brought her, wooden animals and tin soldiers, and again she would cast them from her with cunning energy. I know, she let me stay with her, yet when I asked her what she was thinking, she would say "Nothing." Always she said that when anyone asked her what she was thinking, and in the end, Madame, it produced upon them all a sort of avid forgetfulness of her person, and they would talk openly before her of the ways she would die. And she did not seem to notice; that made it sorrowful and ridiculous, as if they were anticipating a doom that had fallen already a hundred years.

Yet I think Dusie cared for only one of them all, for Madame K—, and that was not liking, it was something else; she loved her as one loves the only reality. You can see, Madame, how that would be strong, inexorable.

Clarissa knew how it was with Dusie, and so she followed Madame K— about, and sometimes touching her for no reason at all, saying I adore that woman! Then Madame K— would go away, and sitting in the music room would play a waltz slowly, too slow for dancing, except in the numbed intervals of sleep. And soon Dusie would be found standing beside her, frowning, preoccupied.

One night it was raining, and Dusie came into the café where I was drinking my coffee, and she came up to me and she said I must come with her, because Madame K— had gone to see her mother that night, and she was afraid to sleep alone. It was very late, it must have been midnight, but I got up, and went with her.

When we got into the big house, and up into the boudoir, she opened a bottle of sherry, and we drank a little, and talked, as we sat on either side of the bed and got out of our clothes, quickly and quietly. And when we were in bed, she began to speak, staring up at the canopy.

"Have you lived here always?" she said, and I said "No, I had lived in many places," and I told her some of the names of the places, Berlin and Holland and Russia and Poland. And she said, "What was in that town?" And I said, "In that town there were beautiful men in shining black beards, and they had sledges and ships and were happy and cold all day, nevertheless one man there had a mother who stole ducks." And that made her laugh, and then she said, "And what was in the other town?" And I said, "In that town there were hundreds of starving dogs." And then she said, "What was the last place like?" And I said, "There were churches there, and the bells rang one way, and every time they rang one way, hundreds and hundreds of old women came through the town and went up the steps, holding their skirts in front, and when the bells rang another way, they all came down again, their skirts lapping the steps, and went away through the town." And she said, "Were there no young people there?" and I said, no, there were no young people there, and she said she would like to go there some day, and be quiet, she always wanted to be where there were old women and animals, and no new life. And I said I wanted to go to America because I was tired of old women and dogs, and she said, "What do you think you will find in America?" And I said, "*Joie de vie!*" And she said nothing at all, and I said, "Is it not so in America?" And she said "No, that was not the way it was." But when I said, "Tell me the way it is with her," she said she did not know. Always so it was with Dusie; at the critical moment she could not explain.

Presently I heard a key in the lock. Dusie started up, and, getting out of bed, said, "Don't come in here. Go to sleep." And went out, pulling the curtain behind her.

For a long time, I heard nothing. I must have slept. Then I heard Clarissa's voice, not loud, but sharp, and clear and sweet, and Dusie's not at all. And I wondered then how is it that Clarissa had a key to the house of Madame, and I thought, she would steal it; it is the only way that she comes by anything. And I knew that there was evil in her visit, and the teaching of evil, and a thing to be done with the heart of Dusie, and I said to myself, "Will Dusie do it?" though I knew not what Dusie was to do, but I feared suddenly for Madame K— and then did not fear because of the way Dusie and Madame K— were with each other always.

After a long time, I head what Clarissa was saying, because I was drowsy and unguarded.

And she said, "You do not look as if you would live long, not long, but I am thirty and I think for you, and you must think too, about the most terrible virtue, which is to be undefiled because one has no way for it; there are women like that, grown women; there should be an end . . ."

I must have slept then, for suddenly Dusie was shaking me roughly and quickly, and I awoke, and I said, "What is it?" And she said, "You must go into the other room and sleep." And I got up, looking for my shoes, and went into the big room and got into bed and forgot. There I dreamed about soldiers and priests and a dog, and people crowding into a thick pack, and the bells ringing, and when I awoke it must have been eleven. The sun was shining in at the window, and the clock had been striking a long time.

I got up to go into Dusie's room to get my dress, and as I came near, I heard her crying, and I went in quickly then and said, "What is it, are you ill?" And she stopped crying, and turned her face to the wall, and someone was turning the key in the lock again and this time it was Madame K— and then I saw Dusie's foot. It was all crushed, and lying helpless, and a trifle of blood ran from the bed to the door and lay upon the hinge. And Dusie said nothing. And Madame K— ran down upon the bed, and took the foot in her lap, and I thought, she will weep now, but she did not weep, she said, "You see how it is, she can think no evil for others, she can only hurt herself. You must go away now." And I went away.

Yes, even now the story had begun to fade with me; it is so in Paris; France eats her own history, *n'est-ce-pas*, Madame?

BEHIND THE HEART

"Now it is of a little boy that I would tell you, Madame, and what he meant for just one week to a lady who had great consequence because her spirit had been level always, in spite of the cost, and for her it had been much, for she at forty had known life for almost forty years, which is not so with most people, *n'est-ce pas*, Madame? Twenty years are given to a child in the beginning on which to grow, and not to be very wise about sadness or happiness, so that the child can wander about a little, and look into the sky and at the ground, and wonder what is to be that has not yet any being, that he may come upon his fate with twenty years to find safety in. And I think with the boy it was this way, but with her it was different, her life was a fate with her always, and she was walking with it when she and the boy met.

"Truly, Madame, seldom in the world is it that I talk of boys, therefore you must know that this was a boy who was very special. He was very young, Madame, scarcely twenty, and I think he had lived only a little while, a year perhaps, perhaps two. He was a Southerner, so that what was bright and quick in him, often seemed strange, so bound about he was with quiet. And she, Madame, she was a Northerner, and introspection hurried her. It was in Paris, Madame, and in the autumn and in the time of rain. For weeks, days and nights for weeks it had been raining. It was raining under the trees, and on the Avenues, and over the houses and along the Seine, so that the water seemed too wet; and the buttresses of churches and the eaves of buildings were weeping steadily; clinging to the angles, endlessly sliding down went the rain. People sat in cafés with their coat collars up, for with the rain the cold came; and everyone was talking everywhere about danger in the weather and in some cafés, there was talk of politics and rain, and love and rain, and rain and ruined crops, and in one café a few people talked of Hess, this lady, Madame, of whom I am speaking. And they said that it was a shame that Hess, who had come to Paris again for the first time in two years to rest and to look over her house and to be a little gay, should have, in her third week, to be taken ill.

"And it was true. Scarcely three weeks, and she was hurried under the knife, so that all her friends were very sorry as they drank. And some said she was very brave, and some said she was beautiful, and some that she was alone always, and some said she was dour, and that, in an amusing way, she took the joy out of life with her laugh. And some of them wondered if it would be necessary to forget her.

"And they went to see her, and one of them came with the boy, that was on the day that she was to go home, and she was not very strong yet, and she looked at the boy, and she put her hand out to him, and she said: 'You will come and you will stay with me until it is time.' And he said, 'I will come.'

"And that is how it was, Madame, that she came upon her week that was without fate as we understand it, and that is why I am telling it.

"Do I know, Madame, what it was about him that she liked? It was perhaps what anyone looking at him would have seen and liked, according to their nature. That was a curious thing about him, people who did not like him were not the right people; a sort of test he seemed to be of something in people that they had mislaid and would be glad to have again.

"He had light long legs, and he walked straight forward, straight like an Indian his feet went, his body held back. And it was touching and ridiculous because it was the walk of a father of a family in the child of the father, a structural miscalculation dismissed when he sat down, for when he sat down, he was a child without a father, from his little behind up he was so small. His hands were long and thin, and when he held her hands, they were very frail, as if he would not use them long, but when he said *à bientôt* to his friends, Madame, his grip was strong and certain. But his smile, Madame, that was the gentlest thing about him. His teeth were even and white, but it wasn't so much the teeth that mattered, it was the mouth. The upper lip was a lip on a lip, a slight inner line making it double, like the smile of animals when it is spring; and where most mouths follow the line of the bone, his ran outward and upward, regardless of the skull.

"His chin was long and oval, and his eyes were like her eyes, as if they were kinspeople, brother and sister, but some happening apart. His were soft, and shining and eager, and hers were gentle and humorous and satiric. Sometimes he rolled his eyes up, so that one wondered if he were doing it on purpose, or if something in him was trying to think of something, and at that moment they would come back again without the thought, smiling and gentle.

"She lay on her great white bed with many lace pillows and pillows of holy embroidery behind her, and I think, Madame, she was very happy and taken aback, for she had known many loves; love of men who were grim and foolish and confident; love of men who were wise and conceited and nice; and men who knew only what they wanted. Now she looked at a boy and knew that she loved him with a love from back of the heart, alien and strange.

"He sat beside her, chin on hand, looking at her long, and she knew what was between them would be as he wished.

"And they talked about many things. She tried to tell him about her life, but what was terrible and ugly and painful she made funny for his sake; made legend, and folklore, and story, made it *largo* with the sleep in her voice, because he could not know it. And he told her of himself, quickly, as if it were a dream that he was forgetting and must hurry with. And he said: 'You like to think of death, and I don't like to think of death, because I saw it once and could not cry!' And she said: 'Do I know why you could not cry?' And he said, 'You know.'

"Then one night he said, 'I love you,' and she turned about, 'And do you love me,' she said, and he came beside her and knelt down and put his hands on either cheek, his mouth on her mouth, softly, swiftly, with one forward movement of the tongue, like an animal who is eager and yet afraid of a new grass, and he got up quickly. She noticed then that his eyes lay in the side of his head, not as human eyes that are lost in profile, but as the eyes of beasts, standing out clear, bossy and blue, the lashes slanting straight, even and down.

"And then, Madame, she said, 'How do you love me?' And he said, 'I love you more than anyone, as I love sister and mother and someone else I loved once and who is gone.' And happiness went marching with a guard of consternation. 'Mother,' he said, 'is beautiful and thin, and though she is quiet, there is something in her she keeps speaking to: Hush, hush! for sister and me. Sister is beautiful and dark, and she sings deep down in her throat "Now I Lay Down My Heavy Load," with her head held back, like that, to find where it is to sing. And when she laughs, she laughs very hard, she has to sit down wherever she is for the laughter in her stomach, and she dances like mad, and when you are well, we will dance together.'

"And then she said, 'Do you love me as a lover loves.' And he looked at her with those luminous apprehensive eyes, and went past her and he said, 'What you wish is yours.' And the moment she was happy, he leaned forward and said, 'Are you happy?' and she said 'Yes,' and she was very nearly crying, 'And are you happy?' she said to him, and he said, 'Frighteningly happy.' And then she said, 'Come and sit beside me,' and he came, then she began: 'Now where is that little boy I reached out my hand to and said, you will come with me, and you will stay with me until it is time.' His eyes were wide with a kind of shadow of light. Her voice was far away, coming from a great distance to him. 'We lose that other one,' she said. 'When we come to know each other, it is that way always, one comes and the other one goes away, one we lose for one we cannot find. Where is that other little boy? He's gone now and lost now—' His eyes were still looking at her with the shadow of light in them, and then suddenly he was laughing and crying all at once, with his eyes wide open, and his shoulders raised and leaning sideways, and she sat up toward him and put her arms around him as if it must be quick, and she said, 'My sweet! My sweet!' and he was laughing and crying and saying, 'Always I must remember that I believed you.' And his hands between his legs pushed hard against the bed, and they knew that she had reminded them of something.

"The next morning she came to his bed where he slept, for he slept many long hours like a child, and she lay down beside him and put her arms over his head on the pillow and leaned to waken him, and his mouth, closed in sleep, opened, and her teeth touched his teeth, and suddenly he drew his legs up and turned sideways and said, 'I dreamed of you all night, and before I dreamed, I lay here and I was you. My head was your head, and my body was your body, and way down my legs were your legs, and on the left foot was your bracelet. I thought I was mad,' And he said, 'What is it that you are doing to me?' And she got up and went to the window, and she said, 'It is you who are doing it.'

"And presently he came in, in a long dressing gown, his eyes full of sleep, carrying the tray with the tea pot and the *brioches* and the pot of honey, and full of sleep he put crumbs and tea in his mouth, holding one of her hands with his hand. So, Madame, to still the pain at her heart she began making up a story and a plan that would never be.

"'You are my little Groom,' she said, 'and we will go driving in the *Bois*, for that is certainly a thing one must do when one is in love, and you shall wear the long military cape, and we will drink cocktails at the Ritz bar, and we will go down the Seine in a boat, and then we will go to Vienna together, and we will drive through the city in an open carriage, and I shall hold your hand and we shall be very happy. And we will go down to Budapest by water, and you will wrap your cloak about you, and everyone will think we are very handsome and mysterious, and you will know you have a friend.'

"His eyes were enormous, and his mouth smiled with the smaller inner smile, and he said, 'How could I have known that I was to be married!'

"And later, Madame, when she could get up and really walk, they wandered in the Luxembourg gardens, and he held her arm, and she showed him the statue of the queen, holding a little queen in her hand, and he showed her one of three boys running; and they looked at all the flowers beaten down by the rain and at the trellises of grapes and pears, that, covered in paper bags, looked in the distance like unknown lilies. Walking under the high, dark trees, with no branches until they were way up, he said, 'How much of you is mine?' and she answered, 'All that you wish.' And he said, 'I should like to be with you at Christmas,' and he said, 'Mine and nobody else's?' And she said, 'Yours is nobody else's.'

"And then they went back home, Madame, and they had tea by a bright fire, and he said, 'You do not hurt anymore, and I must go now.' And she knew that there was a magic in them that would be broken when he went out of the house. And she said, 'What will you do when I die.'

"And he said, 'One word beneath the name.'

"And she said, 'What word?'

"And he said, 'Lover.'

"And then he began preparing to go away. Watching him dress, her heart dropped down, endlessly down, dark down it went, and joy put out a hand to catch it, and it went on falling; and sorrow put out a hand, and falling, it went falling down as he brushed his hair, and powdered his neck so slow, so delicate, turning his head this way and that, and over his shoulder looking at her, and away slowly, and back again quickly, looking at her, his eyes looking at her softly and gently.

"And it had begun to rain again and it was dark all about the candle he brought to his packing, his books and his shirts and his handkerchiefs and he was hurrying with the lock on his valise because a friend was coming to help him carry it, and his hair fell forward, long and straight and swinging, and he said, 'I will come back in ten days, and we will go. And now I will write to you every day.' And she said, 'You do not have to go,' and he answered her in his little light voice, 'I am going now so I will know what it will be like when you go away forever.' And she was trembling in the dark, and she went away into the bedroom, and stood with her back to the wall, a crying tall figure in the dark, crying and standing still, and he seemed to know it though she made no sound, for he came in to her and he put his hands on her shoulders, the thin forearms against her breast, and he said, 'You are deeply good, and is everything well with you?' And she said, 'I am very gay.' Then he took his valise, and his books under his arm, and kissed her quickly and opened the door, and there was his friend coming up the stairs. She closed the door then, leaning against it."

A NOTE ON THE TEXTS

The curious reader will find here the provenance of all the stories selected for this volume. In cases where the author revised her work for later republication, the revised versions are the ones reprinted herein.

As of this writing, all the below-listed titles save the two twenty-first century collections are no longer in print.

Collections of Barnes's short fiction
published during her lifetime:

A Book (Boni and Liveright, 1923)

A Night Among the Horses (Horace Liveright, 1929)

Spillway (Faber and Faber, 1962)

Selected Works (Farrar, Straus and Cudahy, 1962)

Posthumous collections:

Smoke, and Other Early Stories (Sun & Moon, 1982)

Collected Stories (Sun & Moon, 1996)

Vivid and Repulsive as the Truth: The Early Works (Dover Publications, 2016)

The Lydia Steptoe Stories (Faber and Faber, 2019)

The stories:

"A Night Among the Horses," *Little Review*, V (December 1918); collected in *A Book* and *A Night Among the Horses*; revised for *Spillway* and *Selected Works*; included in both *Collected Stories* and *Vivid and Repulsive**

"The Valet," *Little Review*, VI (May 1919); collected in *A Book* and *A Night Among the Horses*; revised for *Spillway* and *Selected Works*; included in both *Collected Stories* and *Vivid and Repulsive*

"No-Man's-Mare," originally published under the title "Fate—the Pacemaker," *New York Morning Telegraph Sunday Magazine*, July 22, 1917; collected and retitled in *A Book* and *A Night Among the Horses*; included in *Collected Stories*

"Oscar," *Little Review*, VI (April 1920); collected in *A Book* and *A Night Among the Horses*; Included in *Collected Stories*.

"The Rabbit," *New York Morning Telegraph Sunday Magazine*, October 7,1917; collected in *A Book* and *A Night Among the Horses*; revised for *Spillway* and *Selected Works*; included in *Collected Stories*

"The Doctors," originally published as "Katrina Silverstaff," *Little Review*, VII (January–March 1921); collected in *A Book* and *A Night Among the Horses*; revised and retitled for *Spillway* and *Selected Works*; included in *Collected Stories* and, under its original title, in *Vivid and Repulsive*

"Smoke," *New York Morning Telegraph Sunday Magazine*, August 19, 1917; reprinted in *Sun & Moon: A Journal of Literature & Art* 3 (Summer 1976); collected in *Smoke*; included in both *Collected Stories* and *Vivid and Repulsive*

---

* These notes are based on Douglas Messerli's bibliography as supplied in the *Collected Stories*.

"The Terrorists," *New York Morning Telegraph Sunday Magazine*, September 30, 1917; collected in *Smoke*; included in *Collected Stories*

"Who Is This Tom Scarlett?" *New York Morning Telegraph Sunday Magazine*, March 11, 1917; collected in *Smoke*; included in *Collected Stories*

"Spillway," originally published as "Beyond the End," *Little Review*, VI (December 1919); collected in *A Book* and *A Night Among the Horses*; revised and retitled for *Spillway* and *Selected Works*; included in *Collected Stories*

"Indian Summer," *New York Morning Telegraph Sunday Magazine*, October 14, 1917; collected in *A Book* and *A Night Among the Horses*; included in *Collected Stories*

"The Robin's House," *Little Review*, VII (September–October 1920); collected in *A Book* and *A Night Among the Horses*; included in *Collected Stories*

"The Passion," *Transatlantic Review*, II (1924); collected in *A Night Among the Horses*; revised for *Spillway* and *Selected Works*; included in *Collected Stories*

"Aller et Retour," *Transalantic Review*, I (April 1924); collected in A *Night Among the Horses*; revised for *Spillway* and *Selected Works*; included in *Collected Stories*

"A Boy Asks a Question," originally published as "A Boy Asks a Question of a Lady" in *A Book*; reprinted in *A Night Among the Horses*; revised and retitled for *Spillway* and *Selected Works*; included in *Collected Stories*

"The Perfect Murder," *Harvard Advocate*, CXXVI (April 1942); collected in *Collected Stories*

"Cassation," originally published as "A Little Girl Tells a Story to a Lady," *Contact Collection of Contemporary Writers* (Paris: Three Mountains Press, 1925); reprinted in *A Night Among the Horses*; revised and retitled for *Spillway* and *Selected Works*; included in *Collected Stories*

"The Grande Malade," originally published as "The Little Girl Continues," *This Quarter*, I (1925); revised and retitled for *Spillway* and *Selected Works*; included in *Collected Stories*

"Dusie," *America Esoterica* (New York: Macy-Masius, 1927); collected in *Collected Stories*

"Behind the Heart," *The Library Chronicle of The University of Texas at Austin*, Summer 1993; included in *Collected Stories*

McNally Editions reissues books that are not widely known but have stood the test of time, that remain as singular and engaging as when they were written. Available in the US wherever books are sold or by subscription from mcnallyeditions.com.

1. Han Suyin, *Winter Love*
2. Penelope Mortimer, *Daddy's Gone A-Hunting*
3. David Foster Wallace, *Something to Do with Paying Attention*
4. Kay Dick, *They*
5. Margaret Kennedy, *Troy Chimneys*
6. Roy Heath, *The Murderer*
7. Manuel Puig, *Betrayed by Rita Hayworth*
8. Maxine Clair, *Rattlebone*
9. Akhil Sharma, *An Obedient Father*
10. Gavin Lambert, *The Goodby People*
11. Edmund White, *Nocturnes for the King of Naples*
12. Lion Feuchtwanger, *The Oppermanns*
13. Gary Indiana, *Rent Boy*
14. Alston Anderson, *Lover Man*
15. Michael Clune, *White Out*
16. Martha Dickinson Bianchi, *Emily Dickinson Face to Face*
17. Ursula Parrott, *Ex-Wife*
18. Margaret Kennedy, *The Feast*
19. Henry Bean, *The Nenoquich*
20. Mary Gaitskill, *The Devil's Treasure*
21. Elizabeth Mavor, *A Green Equinox*
22. Dinah Brooke, *Lord Jim at Home*
23. Phyllis Paul, *Twice Lost*
24. John Bowen, *The Girls*
25. Henry Van Dyke, *Ladies of the Rachmaninoff Eyes*
26. Duff Cooper, *Operation Heartbreak*
27. Jane Ellen Harrison, *Reminiscences of a Student's Life*
28. Robert Shaplen, *Free Love*
29. Grégoire Bouillier, *The Mystery Guest*
30. Ann Schlee, *Rhine Journey*
31. Caroline Blackwood, *The Stepdaughter*
32. Wilfrid Sheed, *Office Politics*
33. Djuna Barnes, *I Am Alien to Life*
34. Dorothy Parker, *Constant Reader*
35. E. B. White, *New York Sketches*